FLORM

Bo...
97...

Bo...
97...

Bo...
97...

Bo...
978...

Bo...
978...

Bo... ...Warriors
97...

Bo... ...e Caves of Pluto
97...

B... ...the Quest for Wisdom
978 1...

Boffin... ...eadly Sw...m
978 18...

Boffin Boy and the Rock Men
978 184167 624 1

Boffin B...
978 1841...

Boffin B...
978 1841...

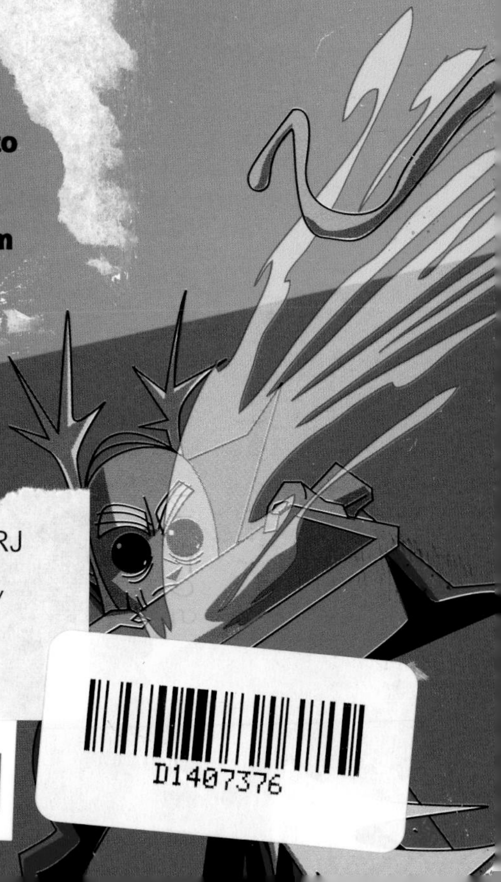

Boffin Boy and the Monsters from the Deep
by David Orme

Illustrated by Peter Richardson

Published by Ransom Publishing Ltd.
51 Southgate Street, Winchester, Hampshire, SO23 9EH, UK
www.ransom.co.uk

ISBN 978 184167 615 9
First published in 2006
Reprinted 2007

A CIP catalogue record of this book is available from the British Library.

Design & layout: *www.macwiz.co.uk*

Find out more about Boffin Boy at *www.ransom.co.uk*.

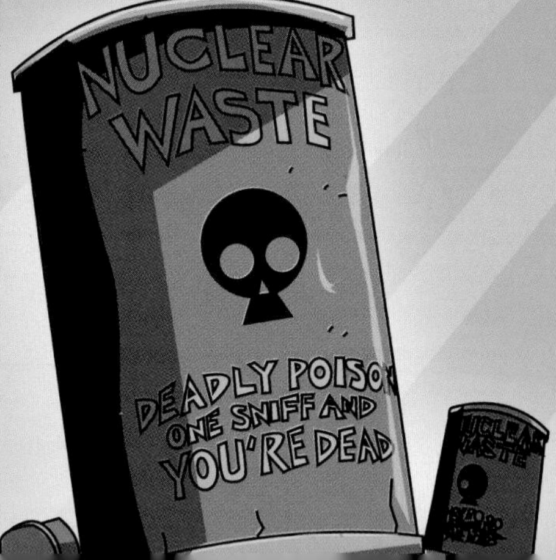
NUCLEAR WASTE
DEADLY POISO
ONE SNIFF AND
YOU'RE DEAD
NUCLEAR WASTE

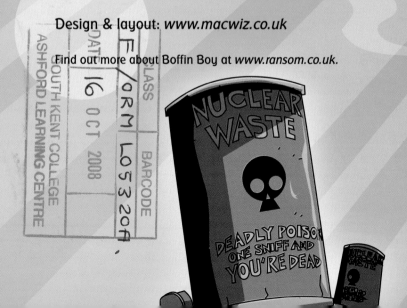

Boffin Boy and the Monsters from the Deep

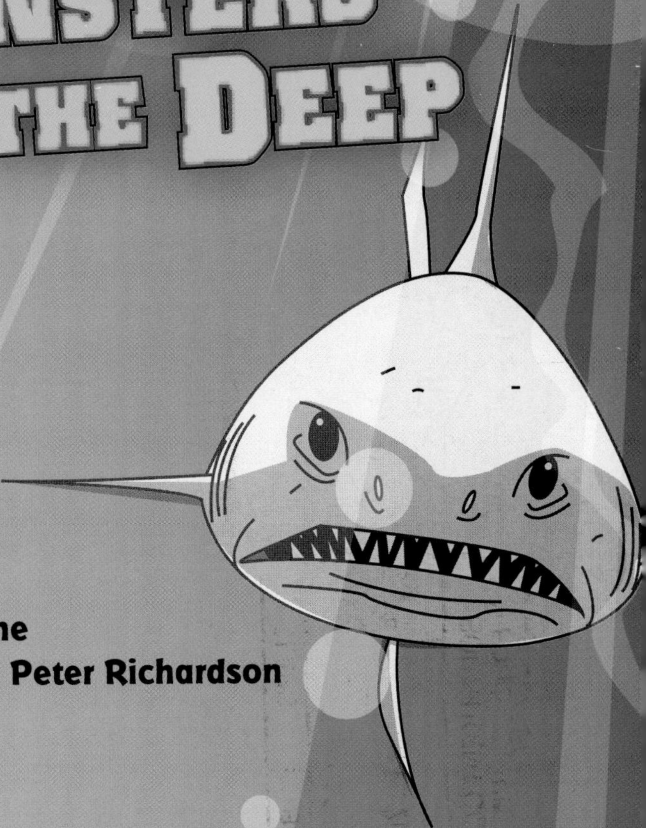

By David Orme
Illustrated by Peter Richardson

Ransom

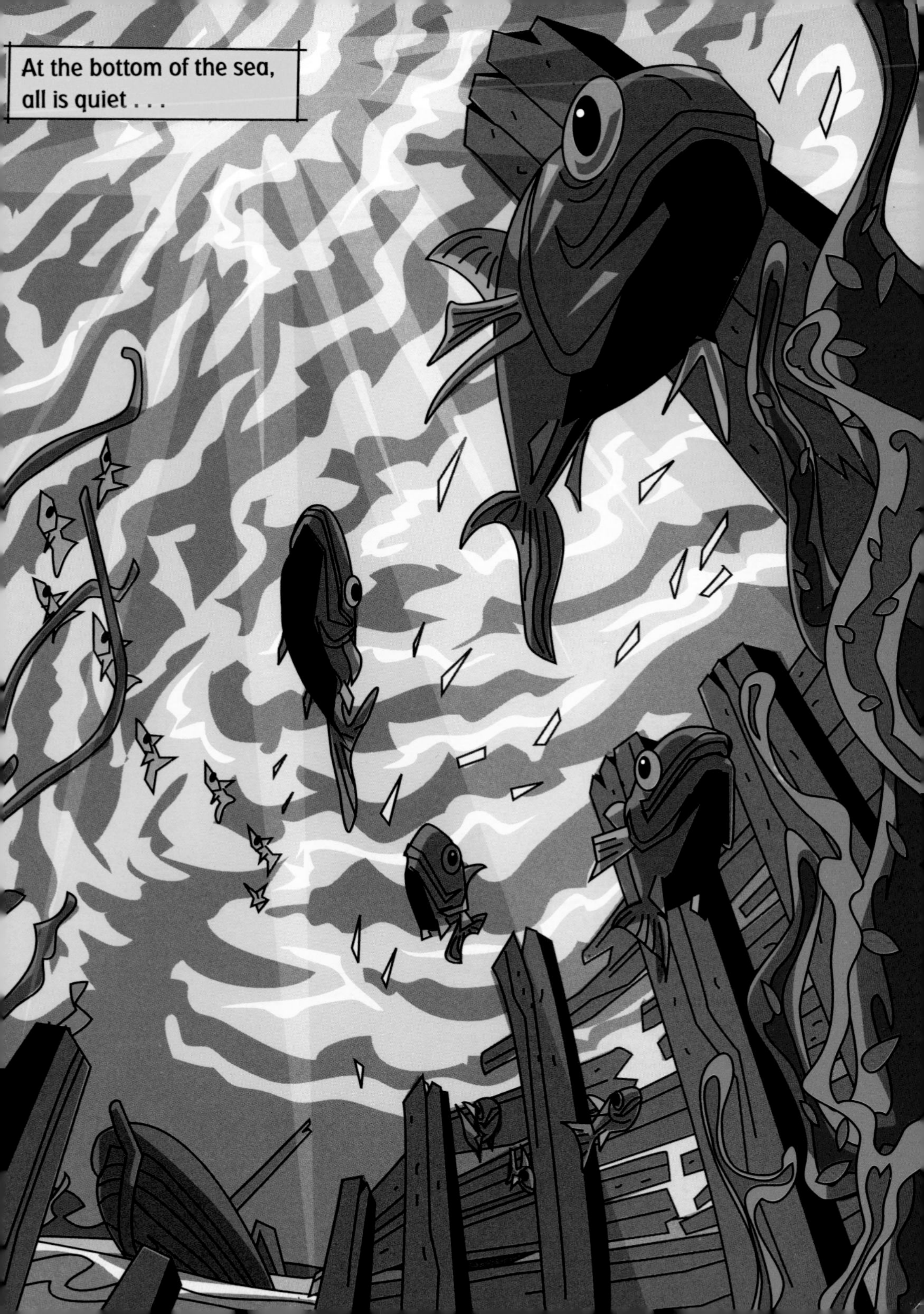
At the bottom of the sea, all is quiet . . .

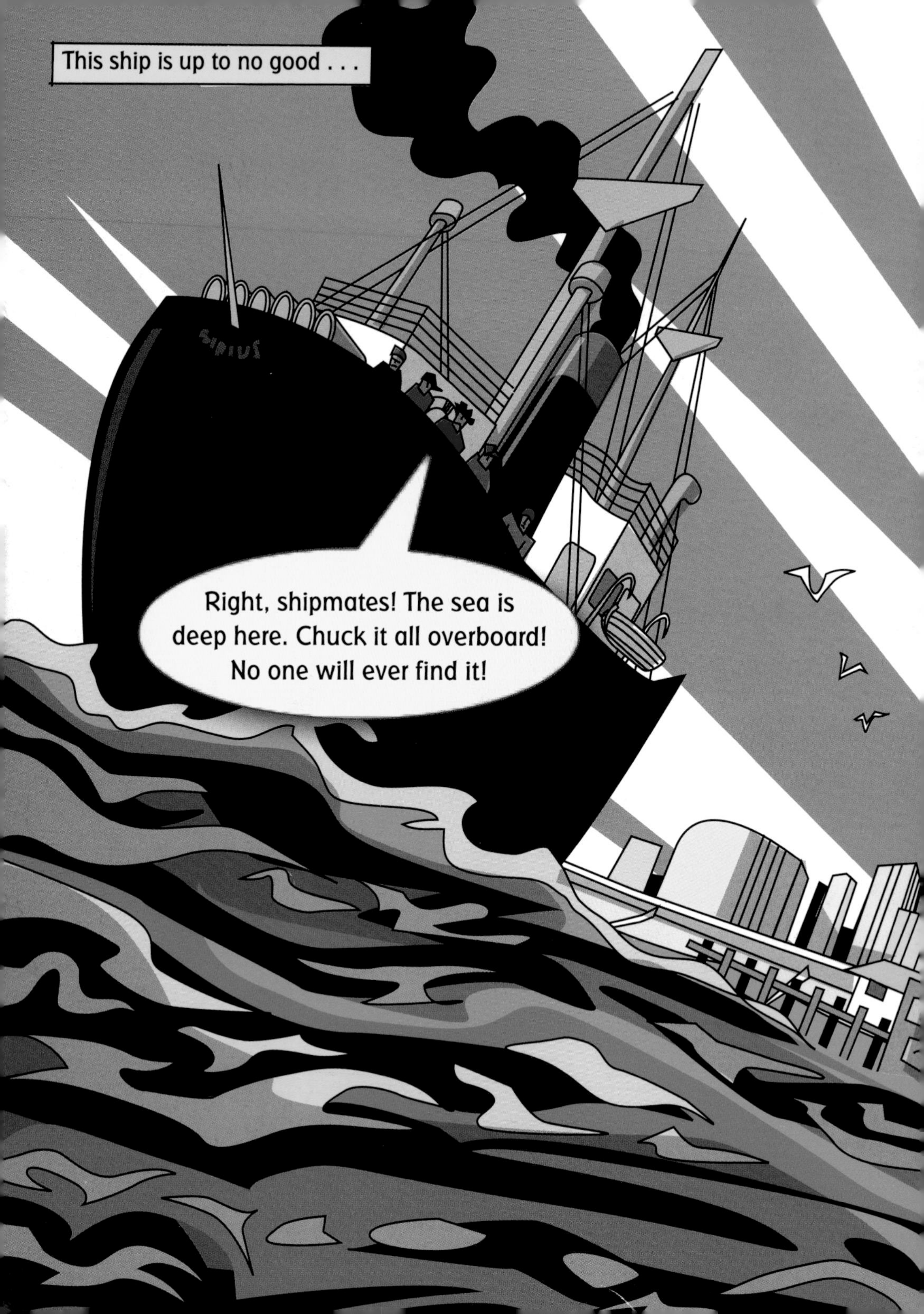
This ship is up to no good . . .
Right, shipmates! The sea is deep here. Chuck it all overboard! No one will ever find it!

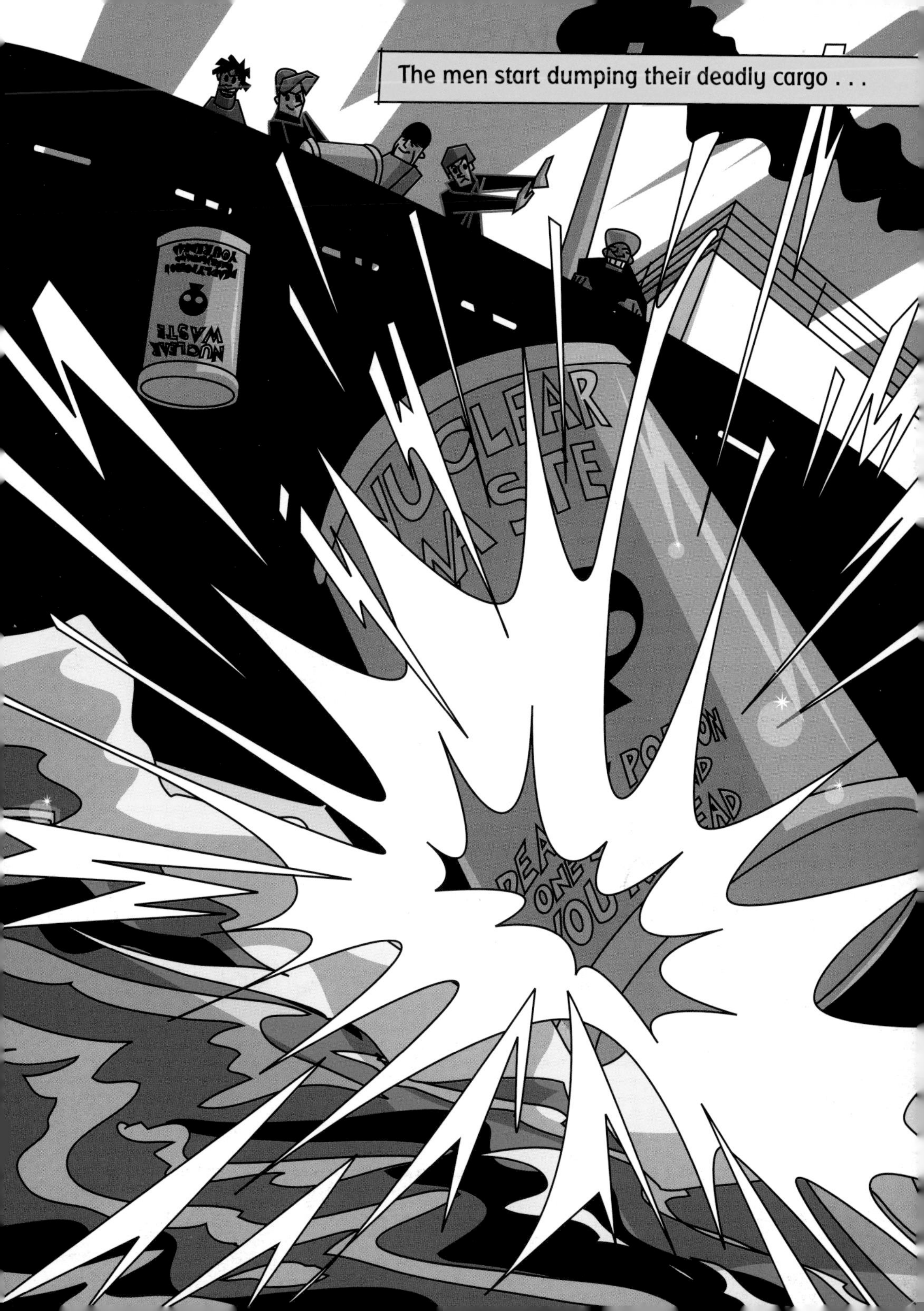
The men start dumping their deadly cargo . . .
NUCLEAR WASTE

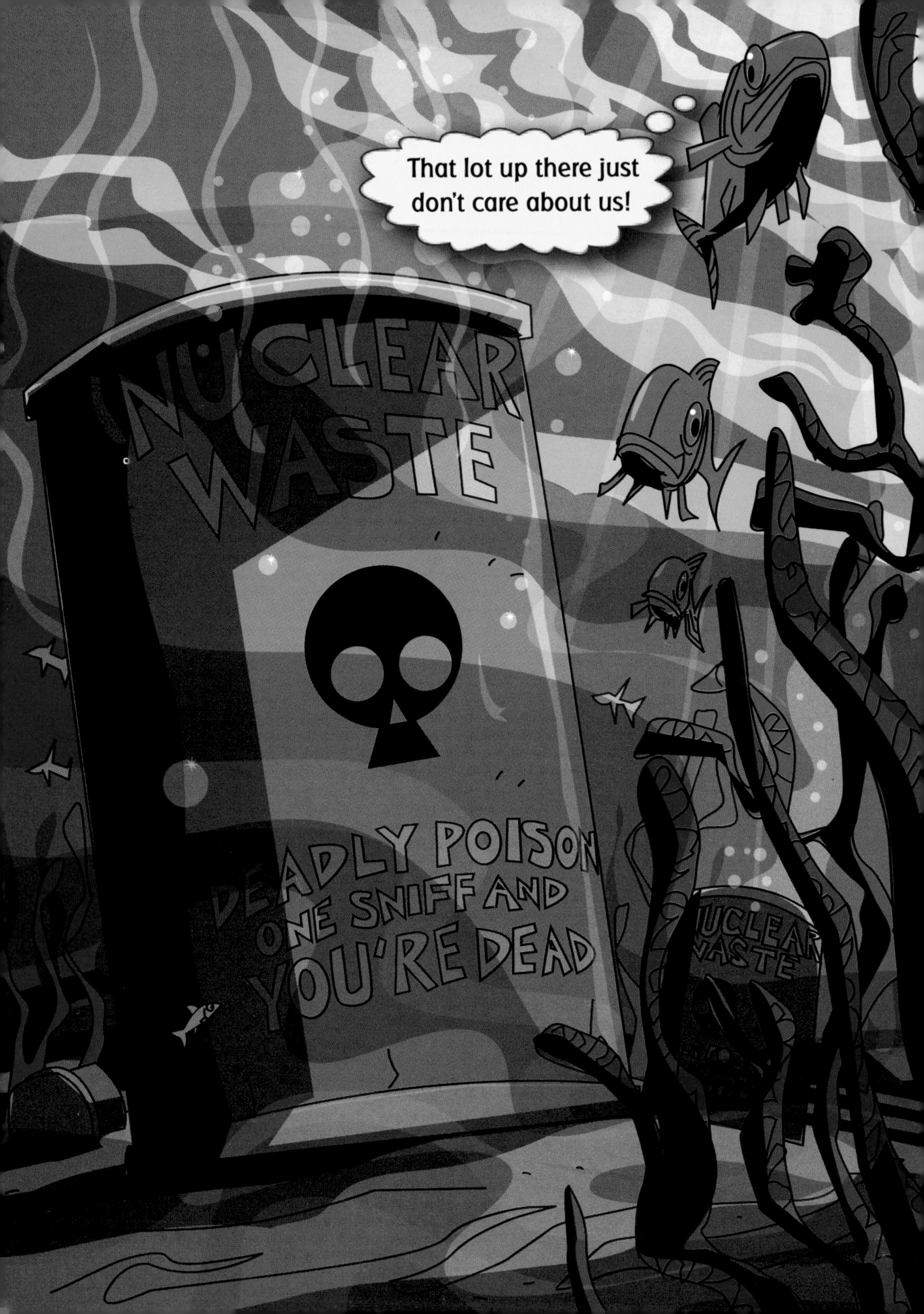
That lot up there just don't care about us!
NUCLEAR WASTE
DEADLY POISON
ONE SNIFF AND
YOU'RE DEAD
NUCLEAR WASTE

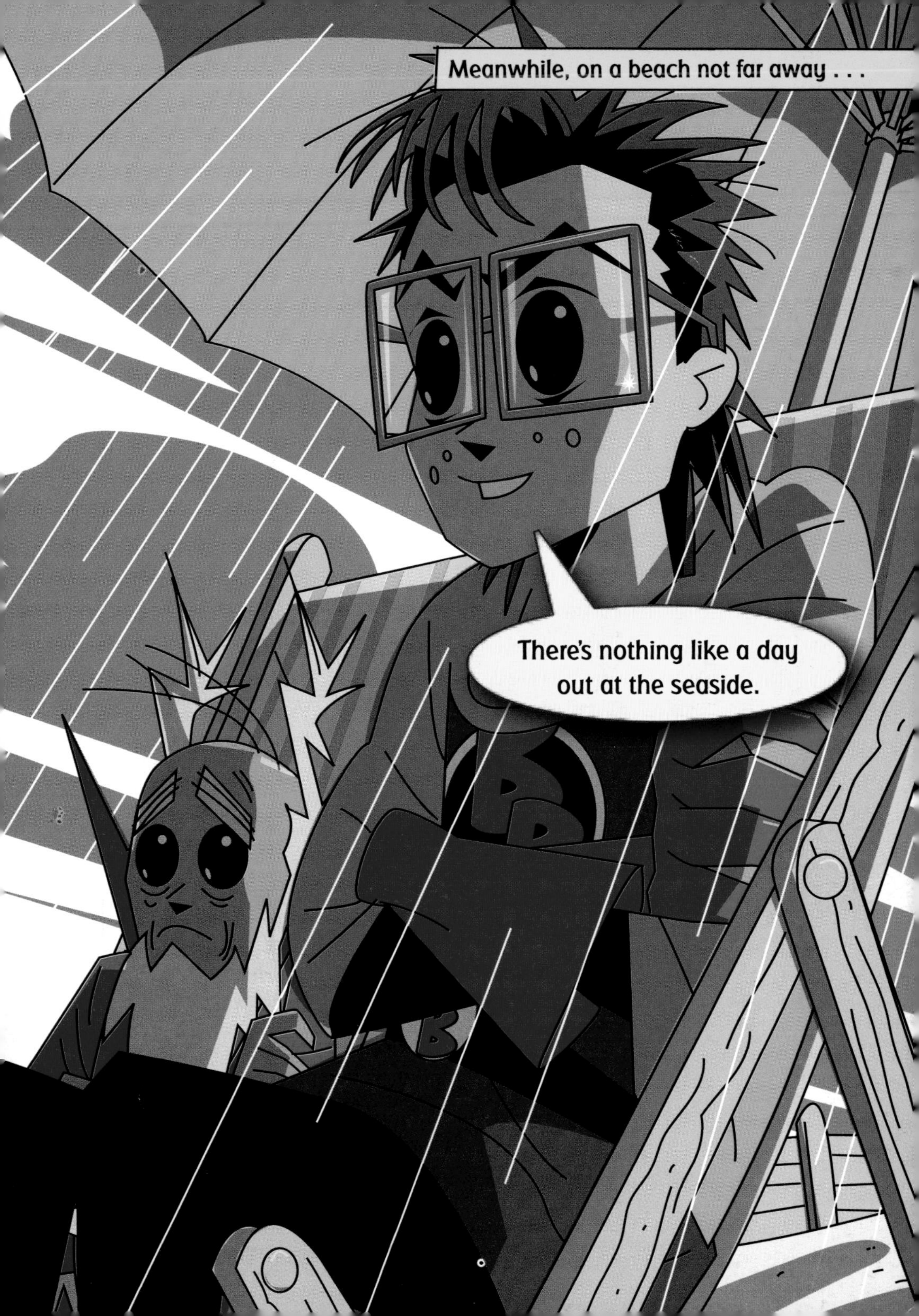
Meanwhile, on a beach not far away . . .
There's nothing like a day out at the seaside.

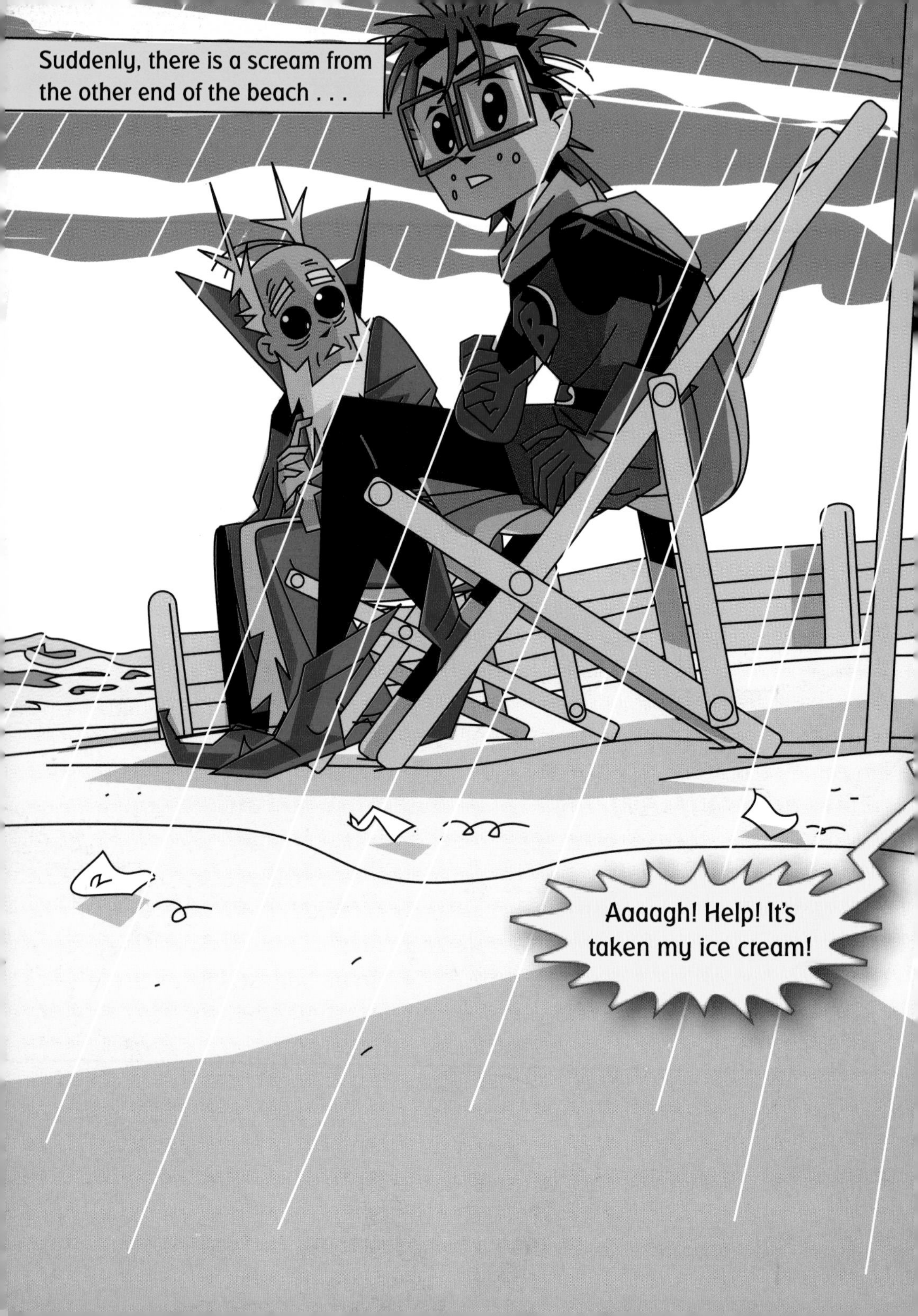
Suddenly, there is a scream from the other end of the beach . . .
Aaaagh! Help! It's taken my ice cream!

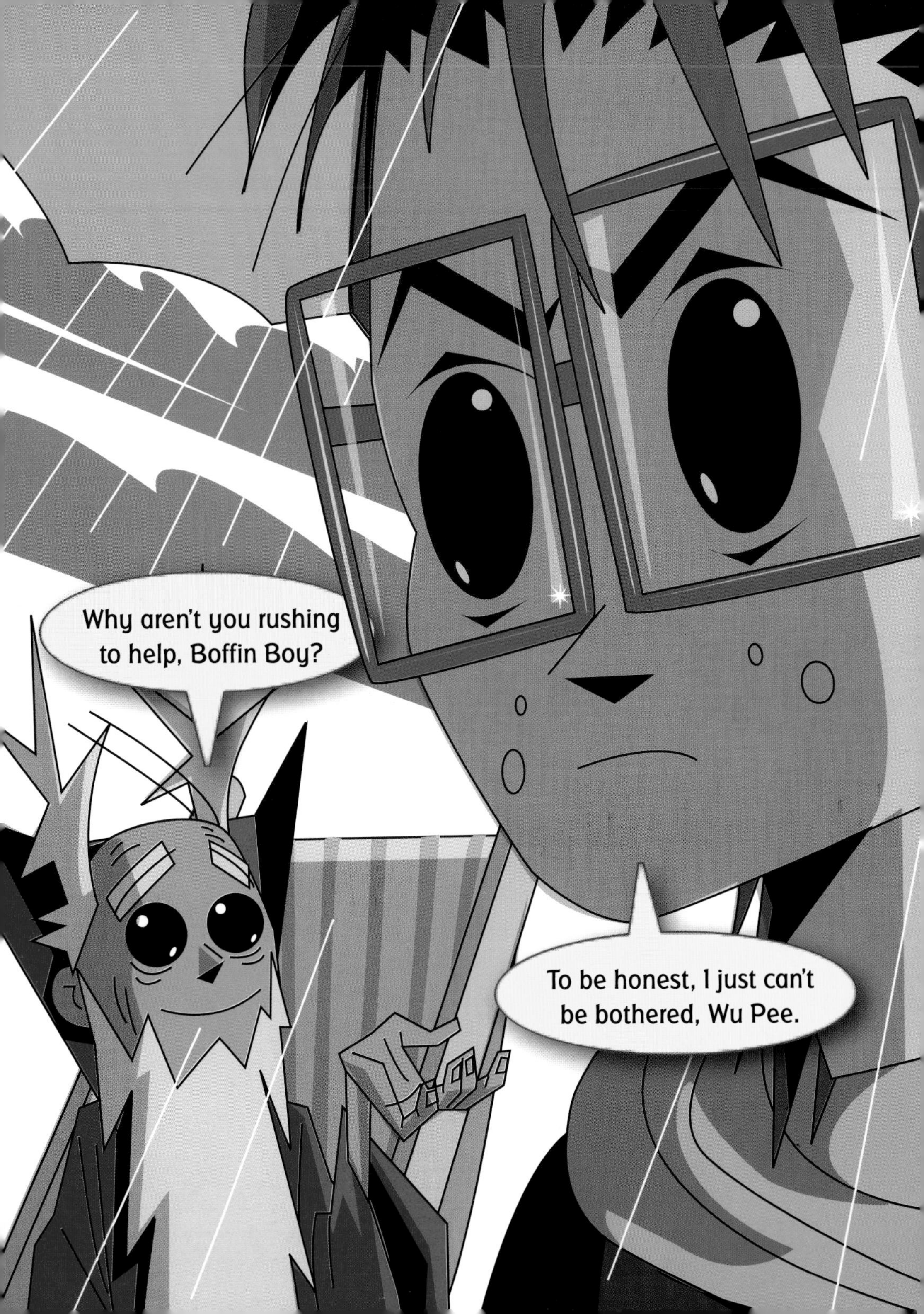
Why aren't you rushing to help, Boffin Boy?
To be honest, I just can't be bothered, Wu Pee.

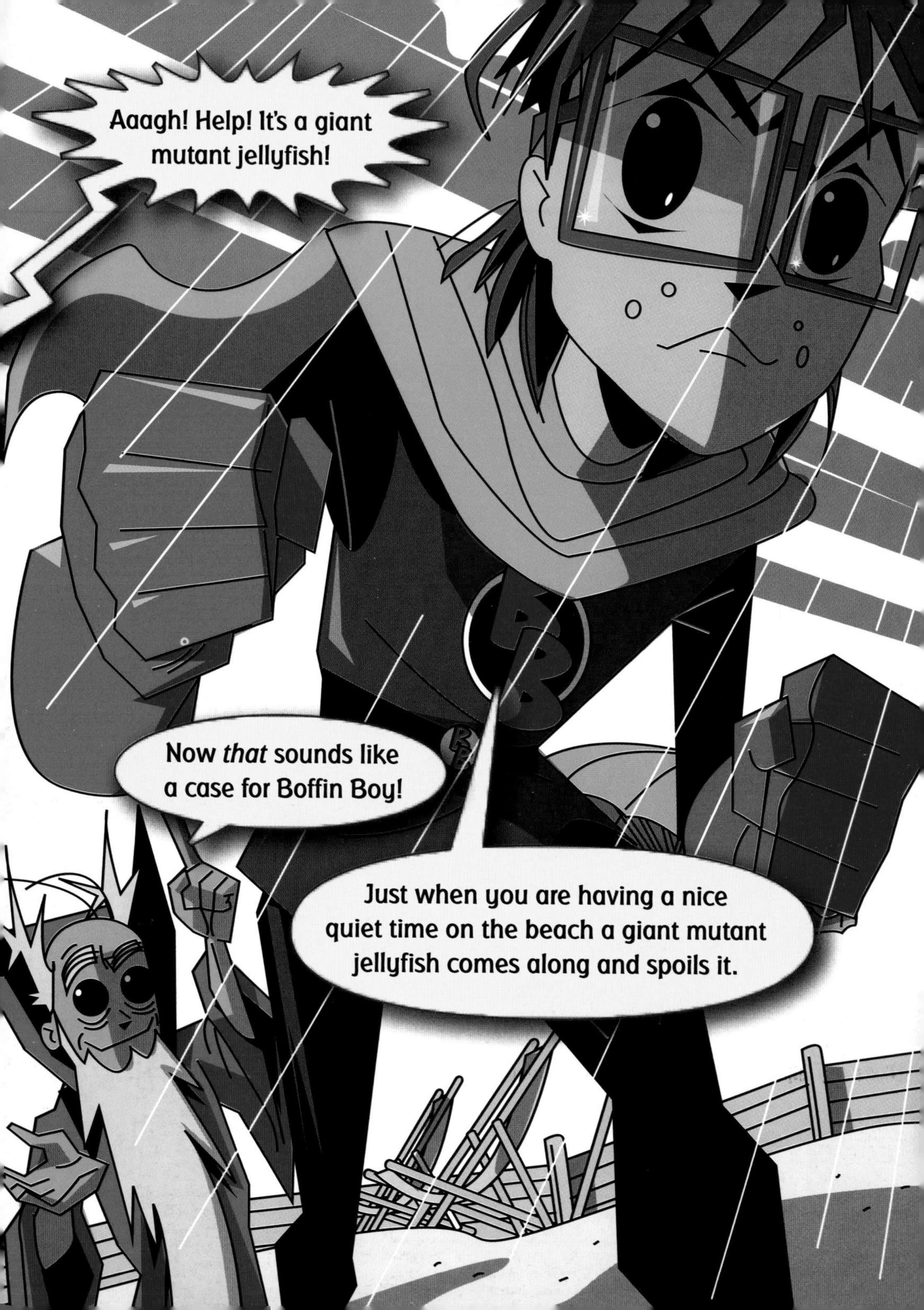
Aaagh! Help! It's a giant mutant jellyfish!
Now *that* sounds like a case for Boffin Boy!
Just when you are having a nice quiet time on the beach a giant mutant jellyfish comes along and spoils it.

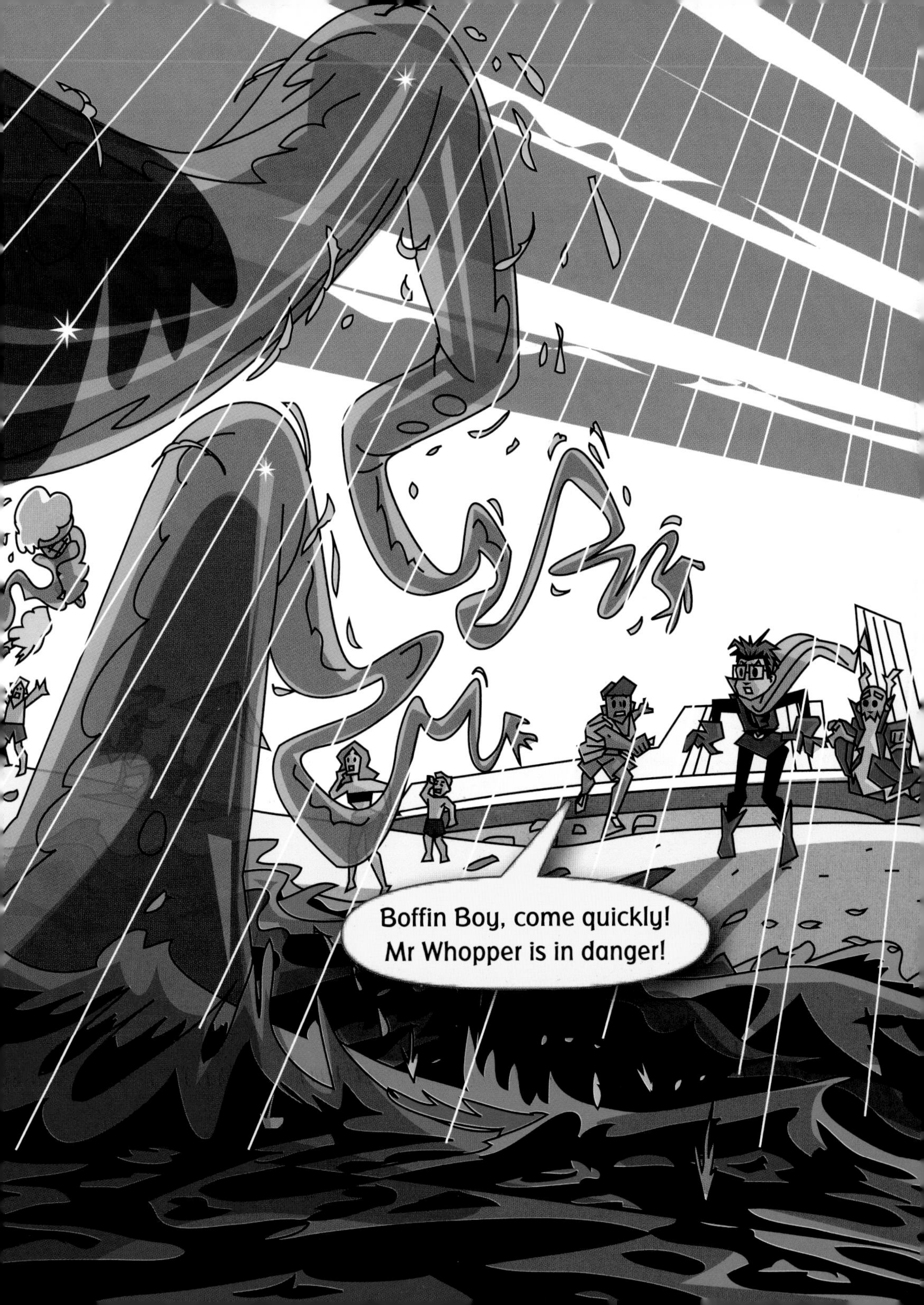
Boffin Boy, come quickly!
Mr Whopper is in danger!

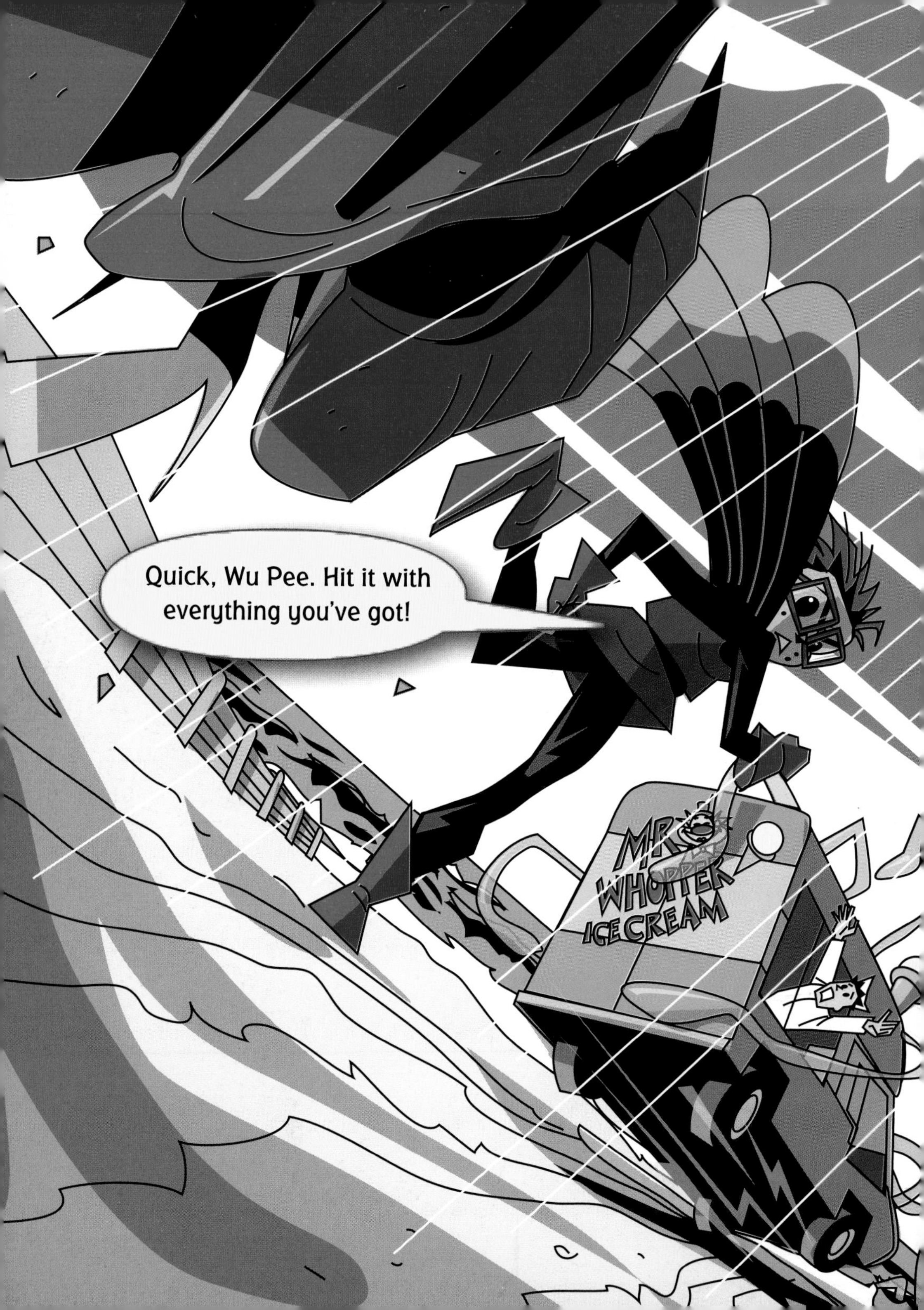
Quick, Wu Pee. Hit it with everything you've got!
MR WHOPPER WHOPPER ICE CREAM

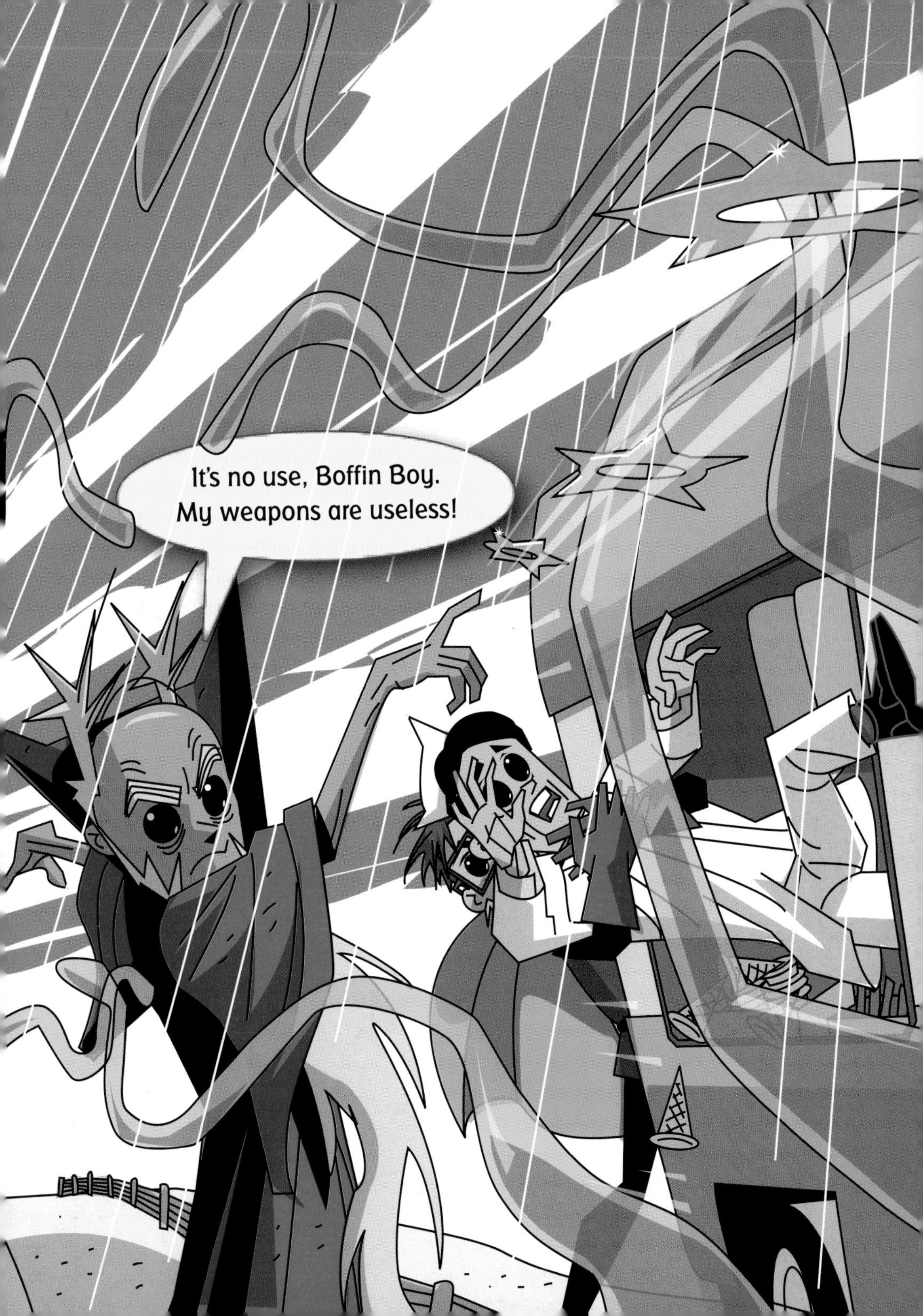
It's no use, Boffin Boy.
My weapons are useless!

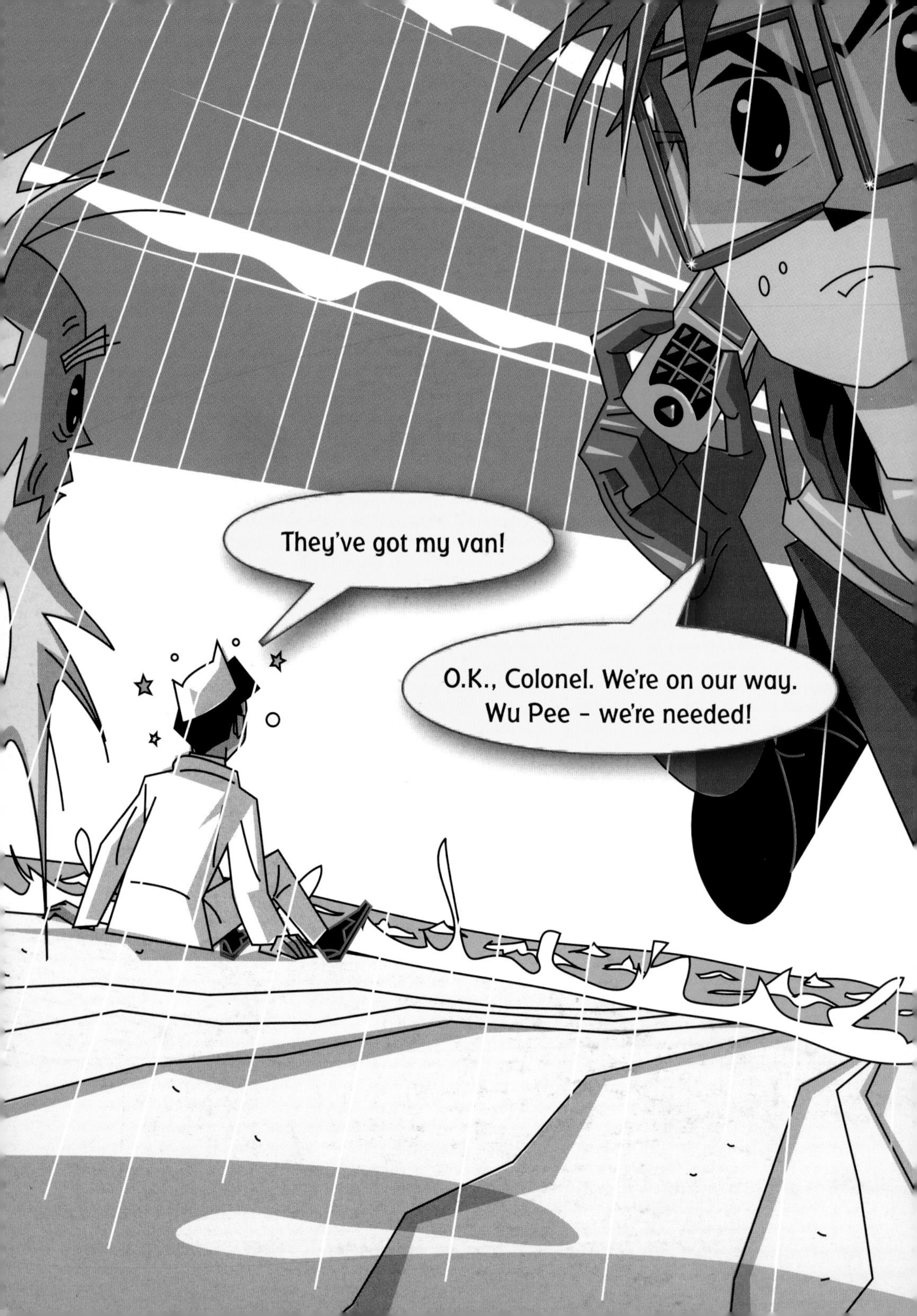
They've got my van!
O.K., Colonel. We're on our way. Wu Pee – we're needed!

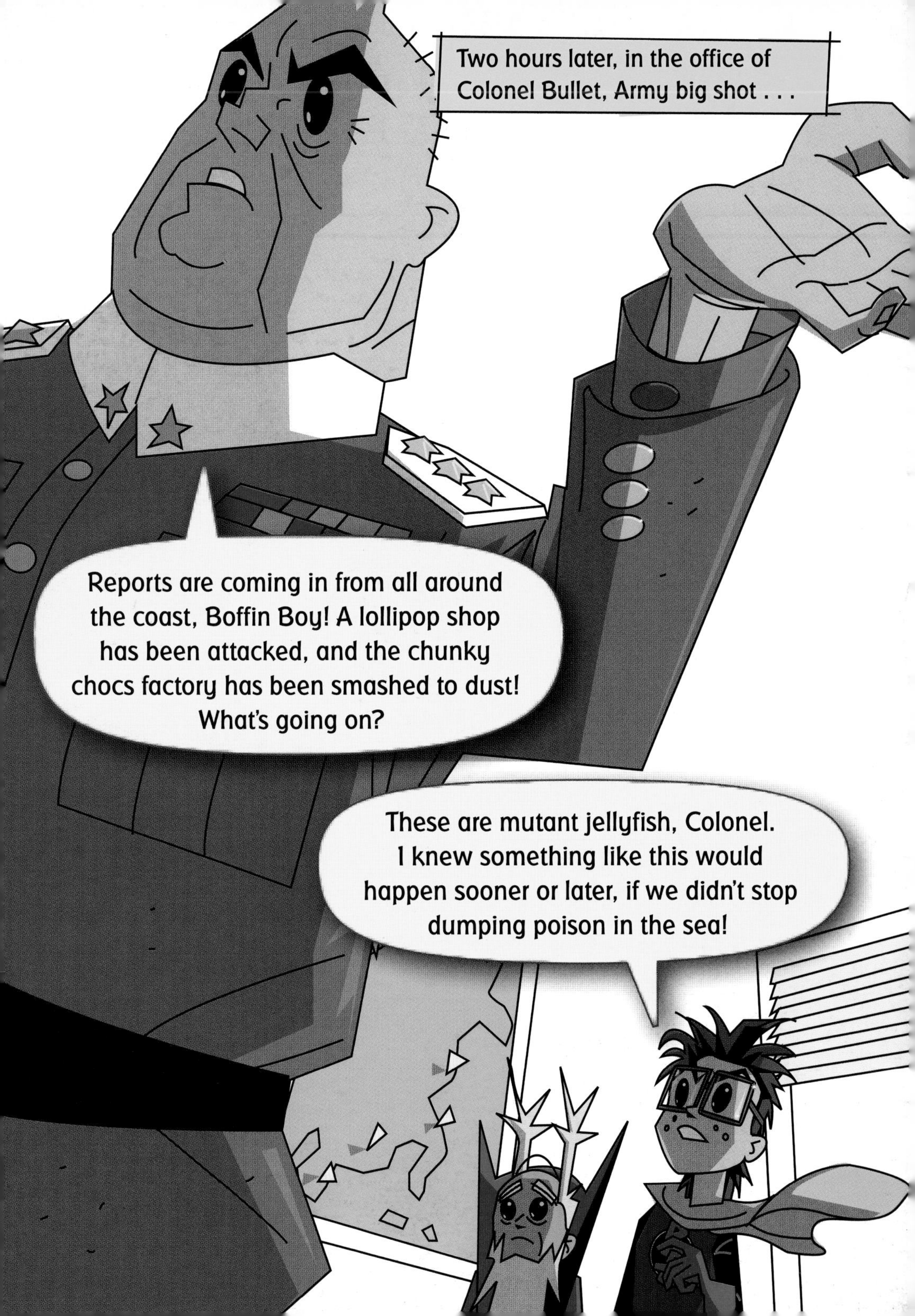
Two hours later, in the office of Colonel Bullet, Army big shot . . .
Reports are coming in from all around the coast, Boffin Boy! A lollipop shop has been attacked, and the chunky chocs factory has been smashed to dust! What's going on?
These are mutant jellyfish, Colonel. I knew something like this would happen sooner or later, if we didn't stop dumping poison in the sea!

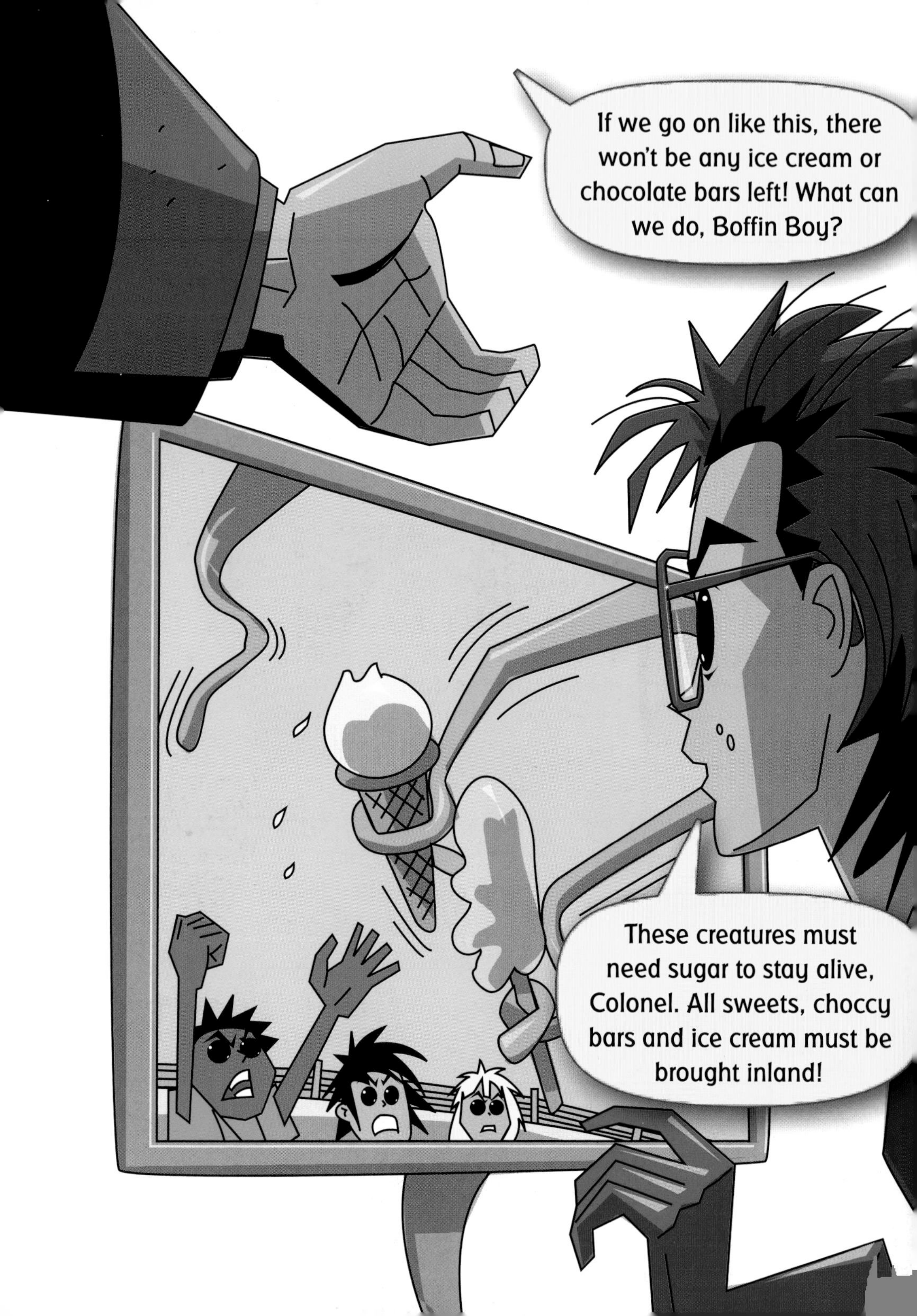
If we go on like this, there won't be any ice cream or chocolate bars left! What can we do, Boffin Boy?
These creatures must need sugar to stay alive, Colonel. All sweets, choccy bars and ice cream must be brought inland!

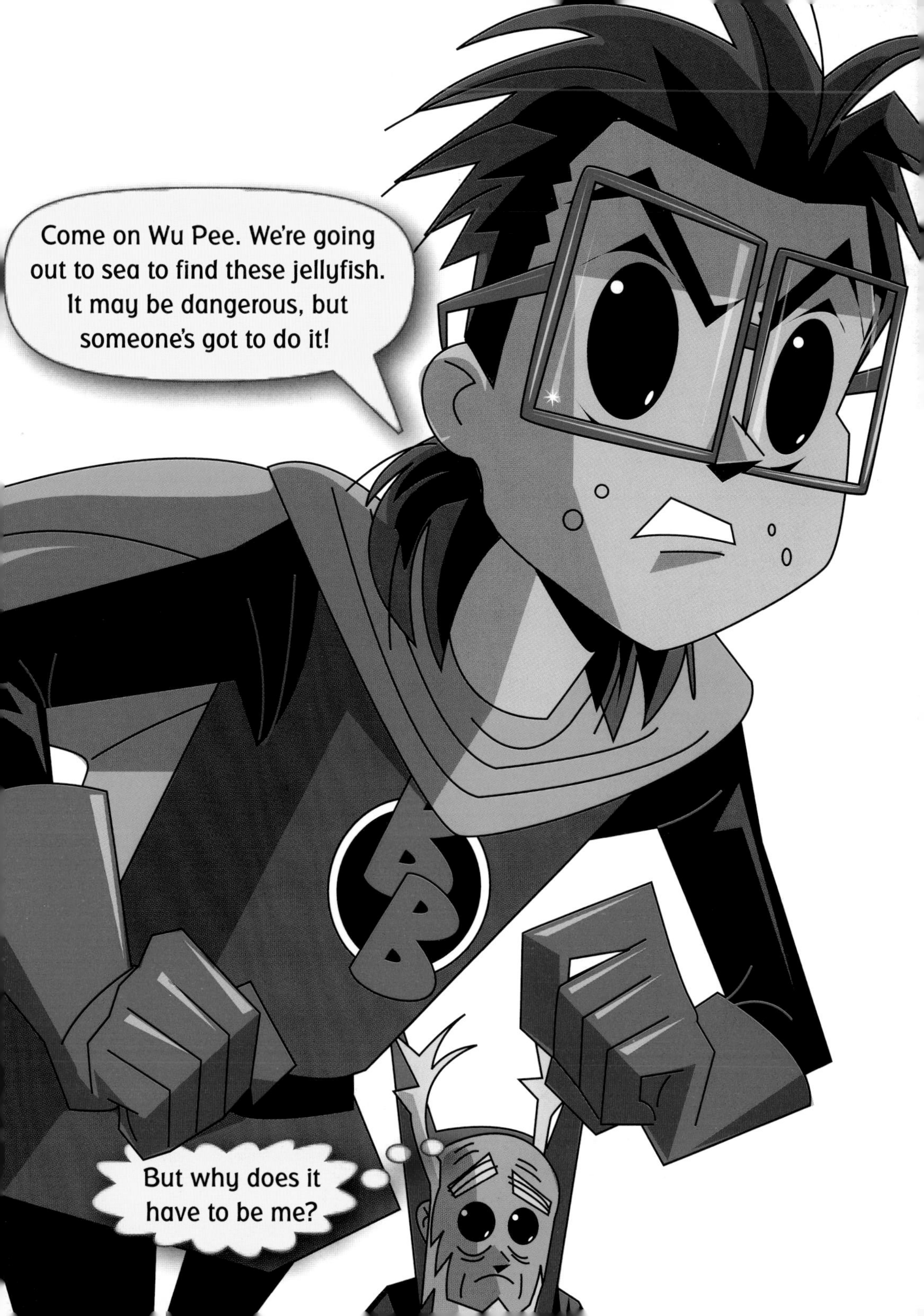
Come on Wu Pee. We're going out to sea to find these jellyfish. It may be dangerous, but someone's got to do it!
But why does it have to be me?

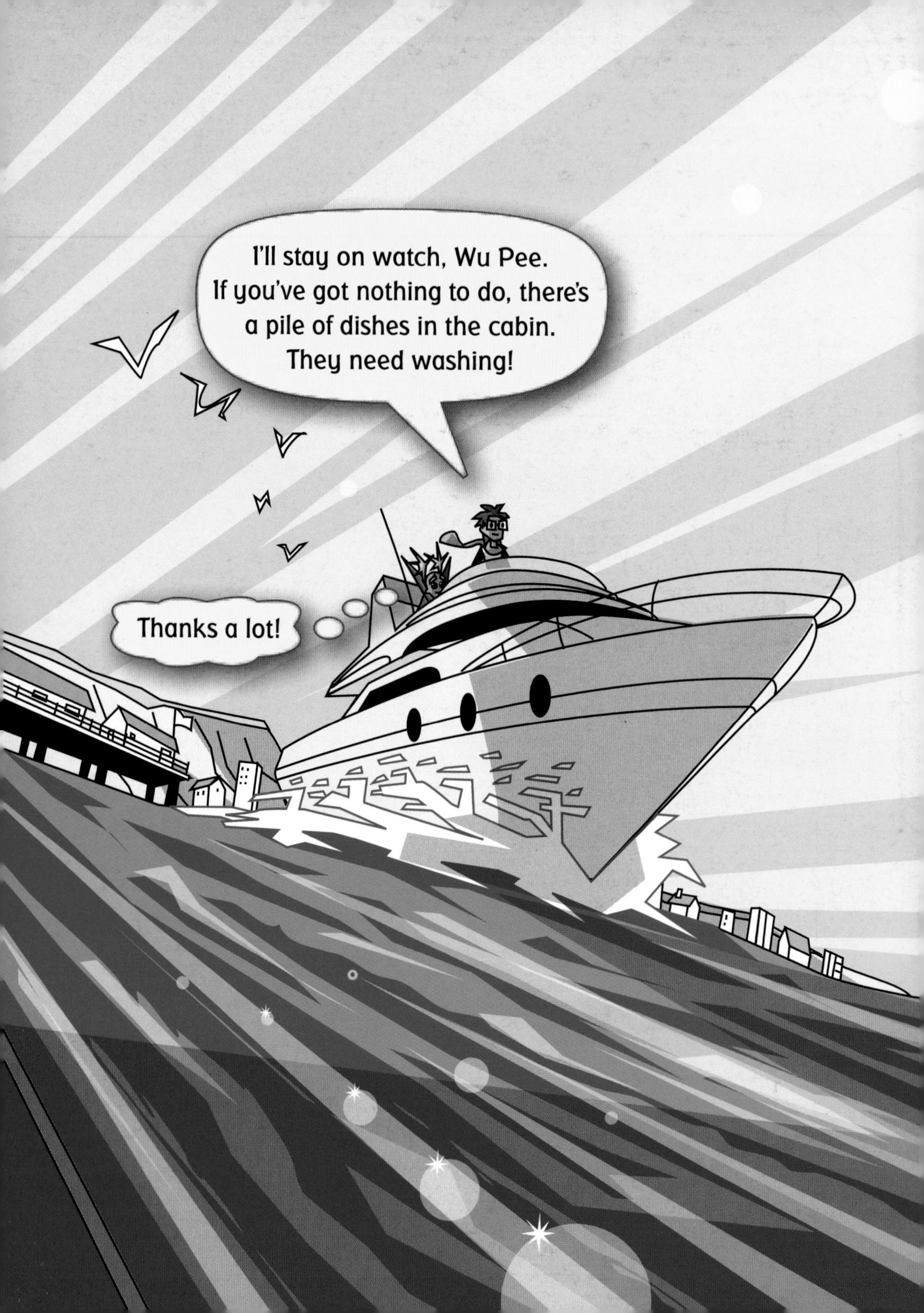
I'll stay on watch, Wu Pee. If you've got nothing to do, there's a pile of dishes in the cabin. They need washing!
Thanks a lot!

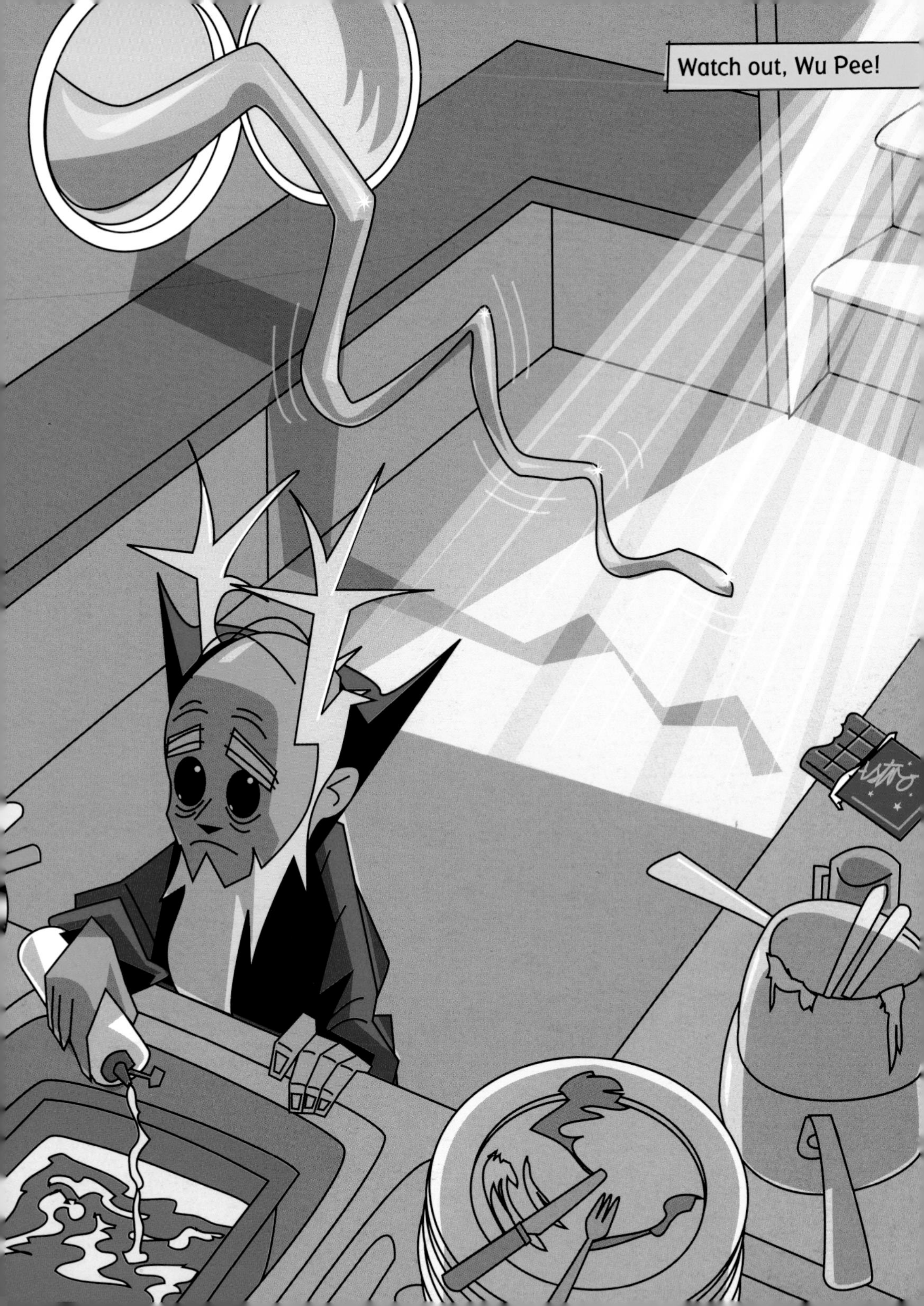
Watch out, Wu Pee!

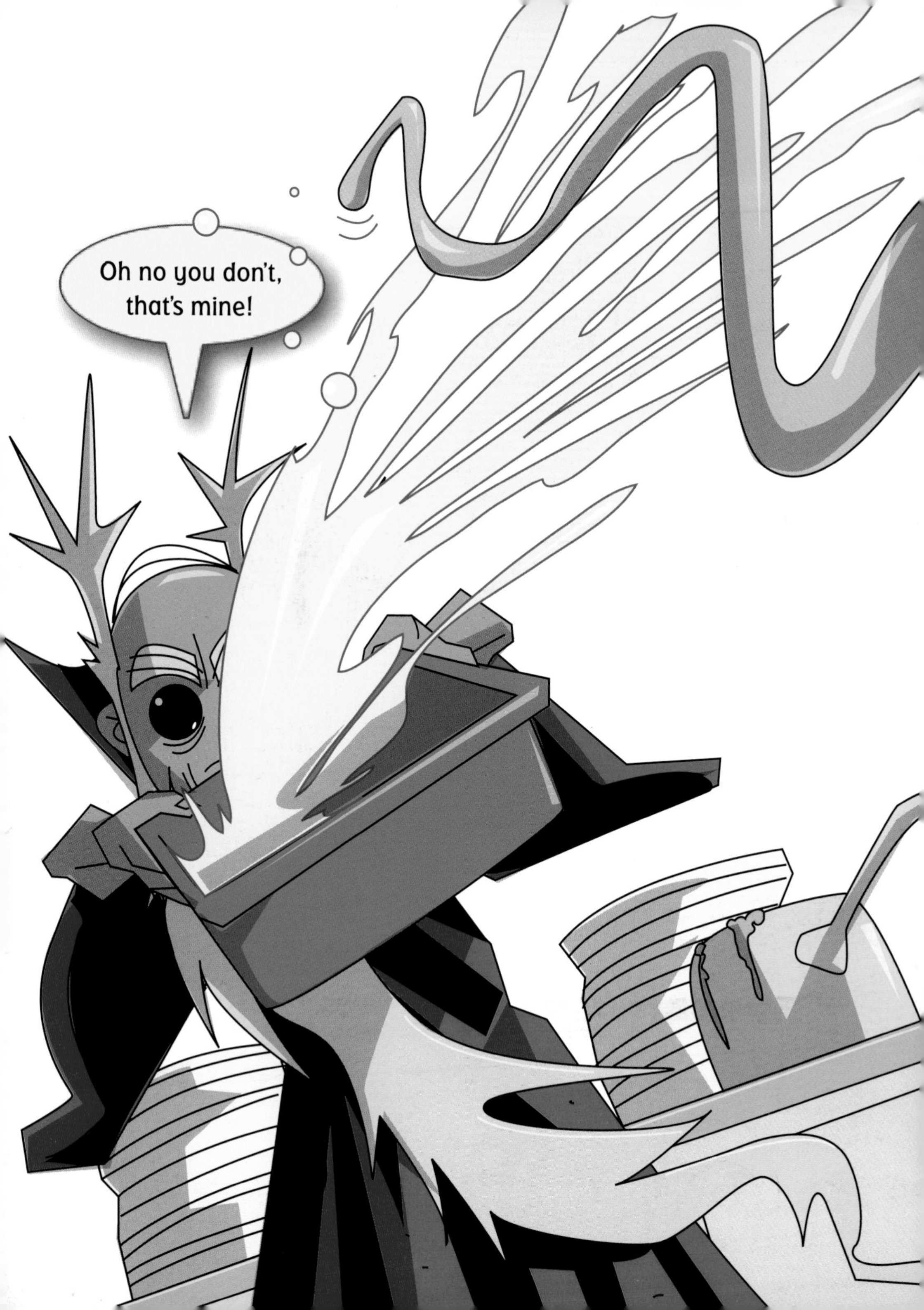
Oh no you don't, that's mine!

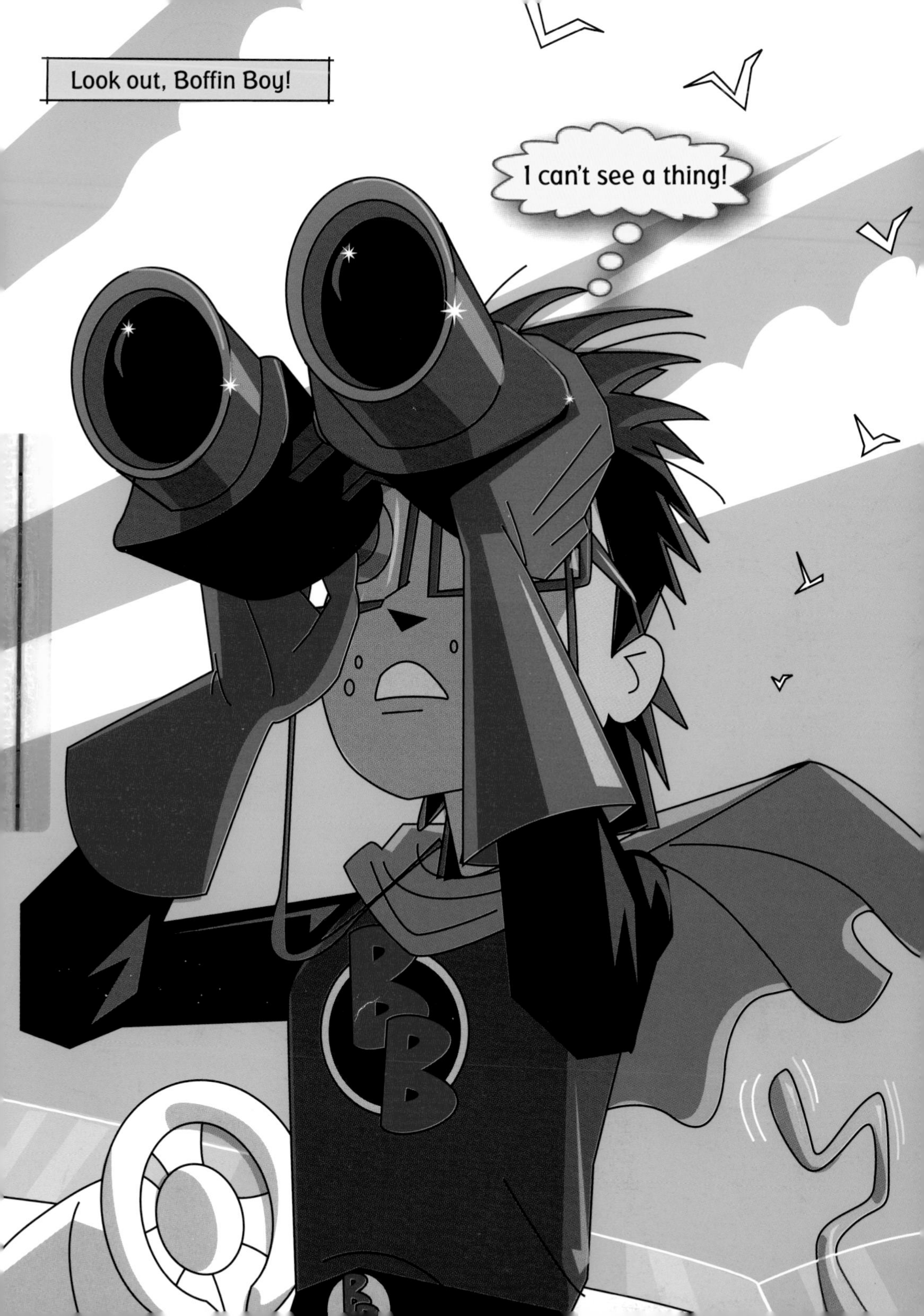
Look out, Boffin Boy!
I can't see a thing!

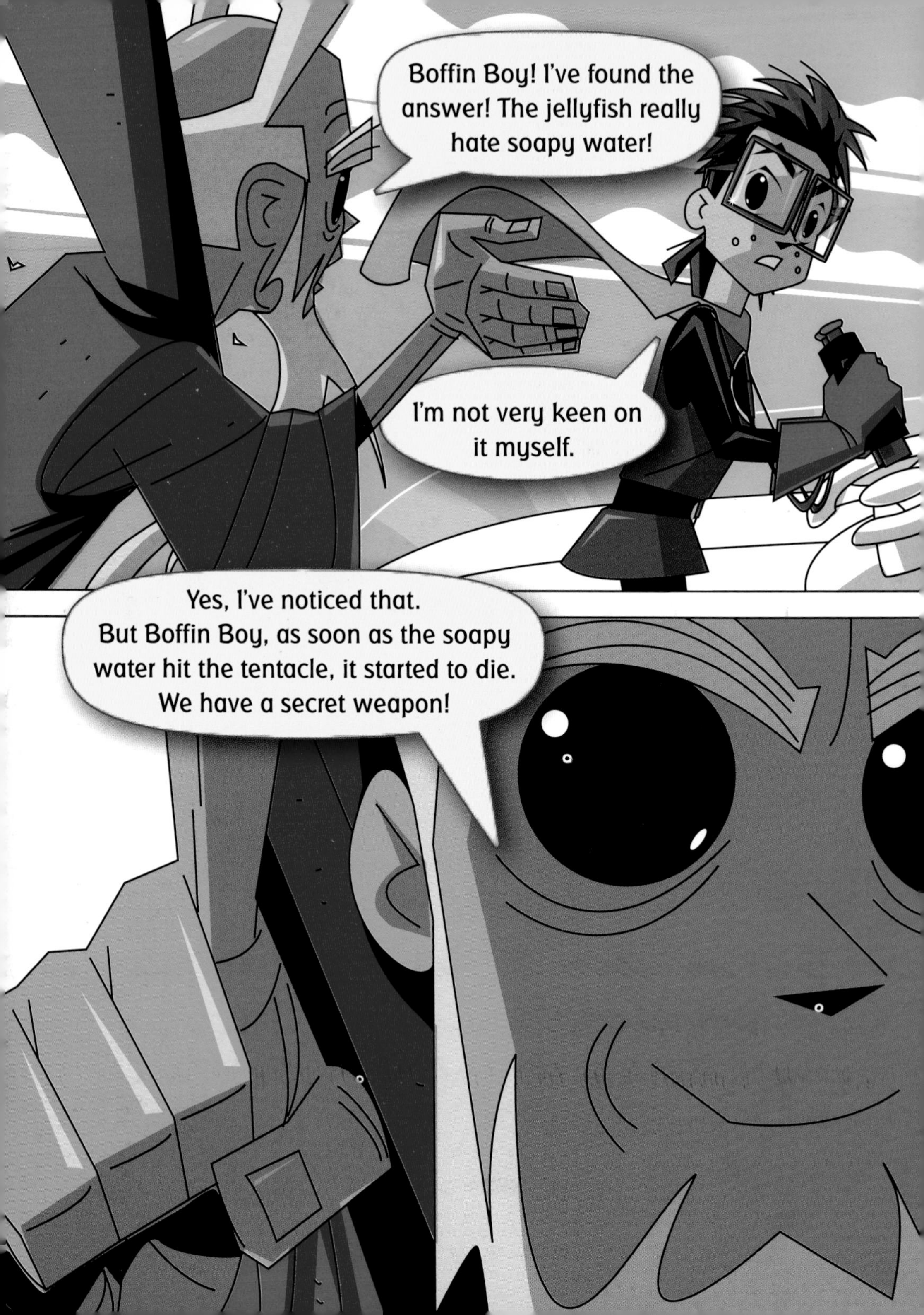
Boffin Boy! I've found the answer! The jellyfish really hate soapy water!
I'm not very keen on it myself.
Yes, I've noticed that. But Boffin Boy, as soon as the soapy water hit the tentacle, it started to die. We have a secret weapon!

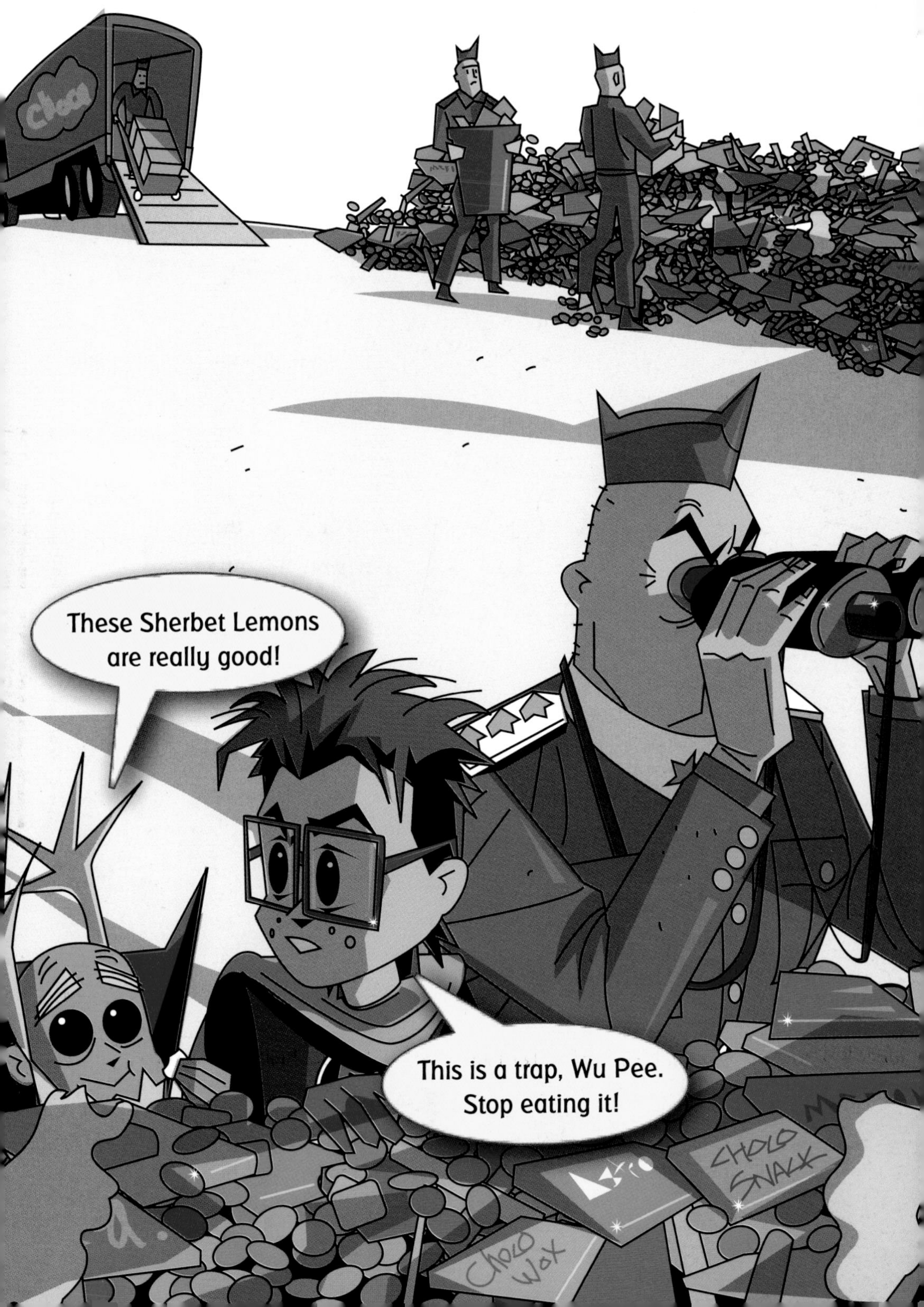

Choco
These Sherbet Lemons are really good!
This is a trap, Wu Pee. Stop eating it!
CHOCO SNACK
CHOCO WOX

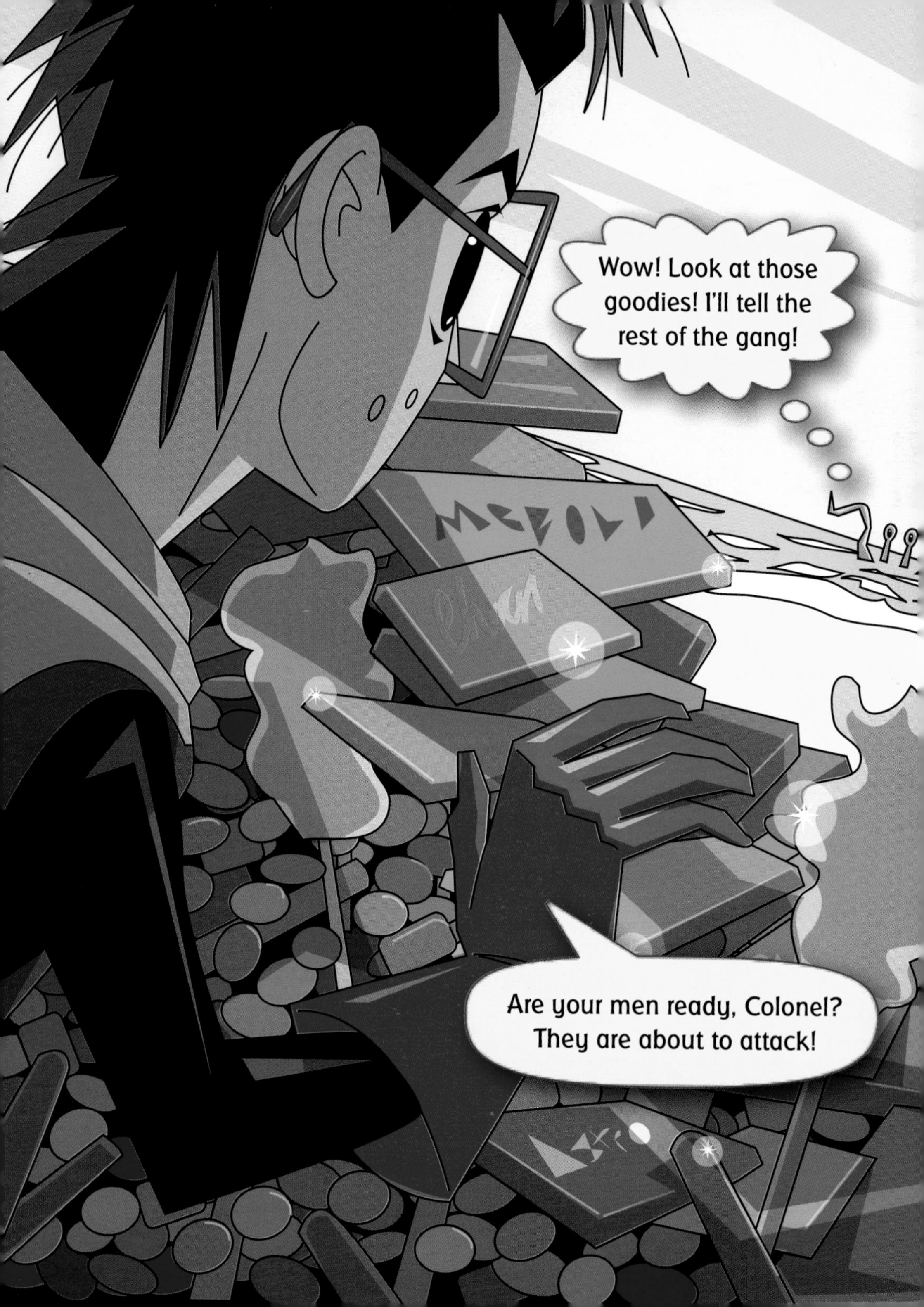
Wow! Look at those goodies! I'll tell the rest of the gang!
Are your men ready, Colonel? They are about to attack!

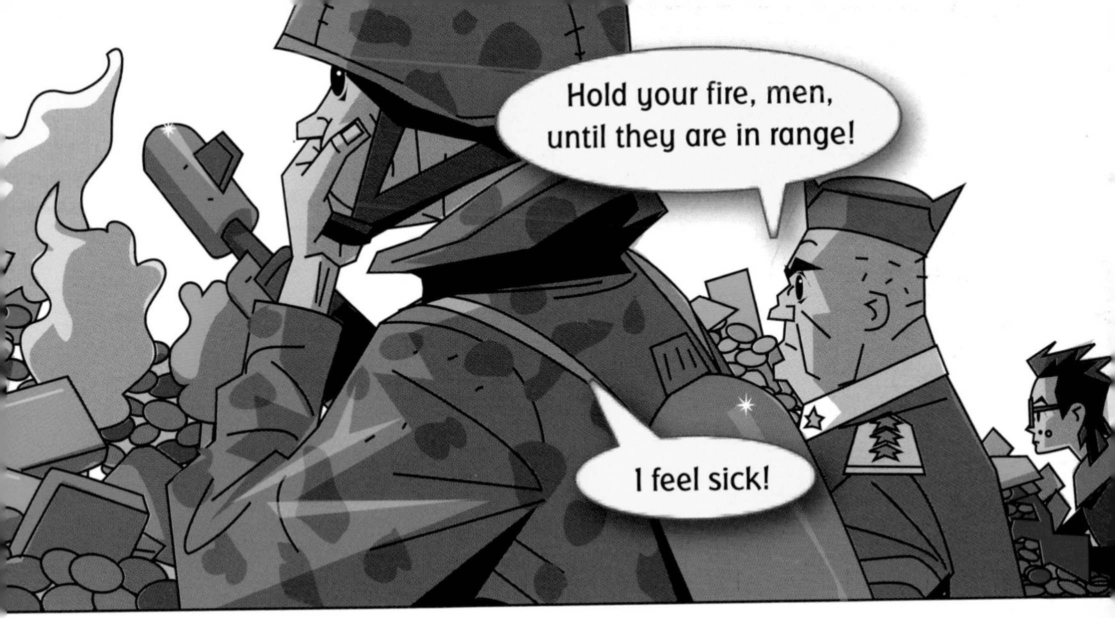
Hold your fire, men, until they are in range!
I feel sick!

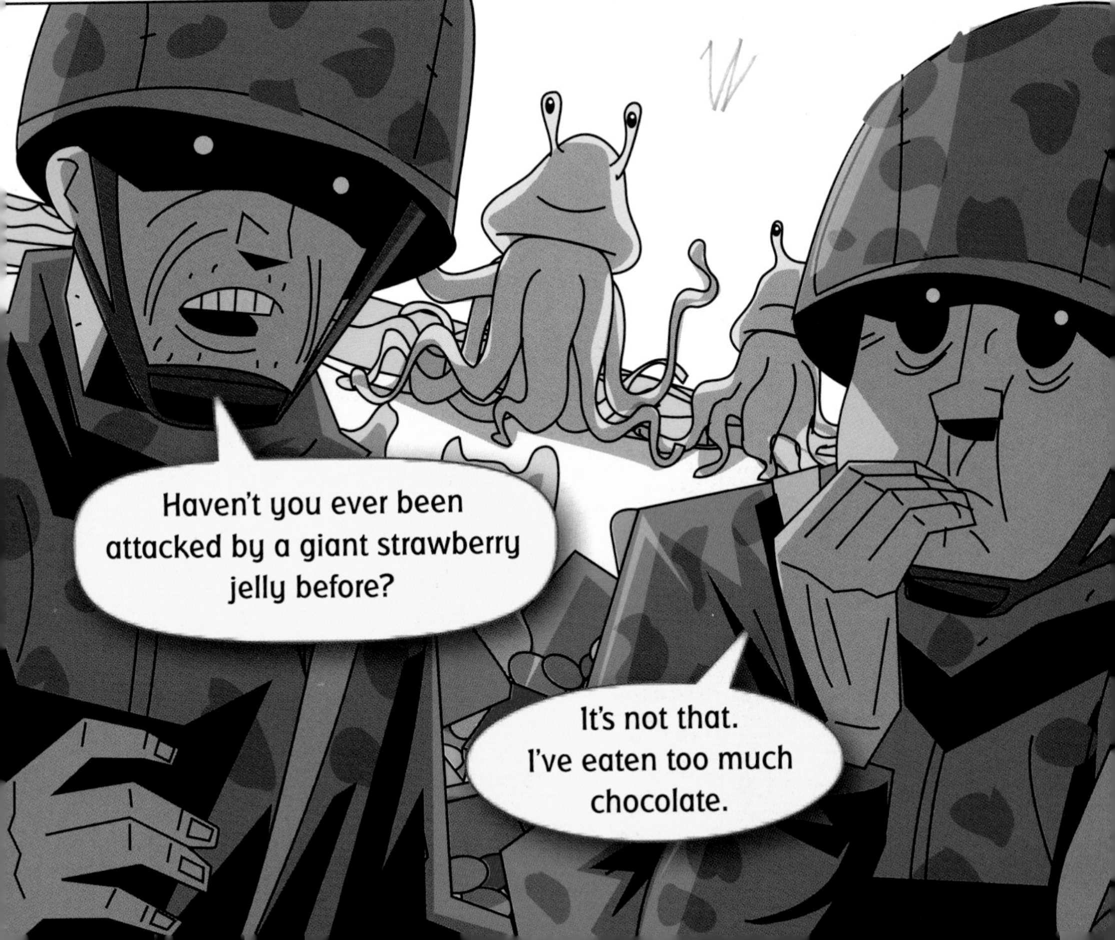
Haven't you ever been attacked by a giant strawberry jelly before?
It's not that. I've eaten too much chocolate.

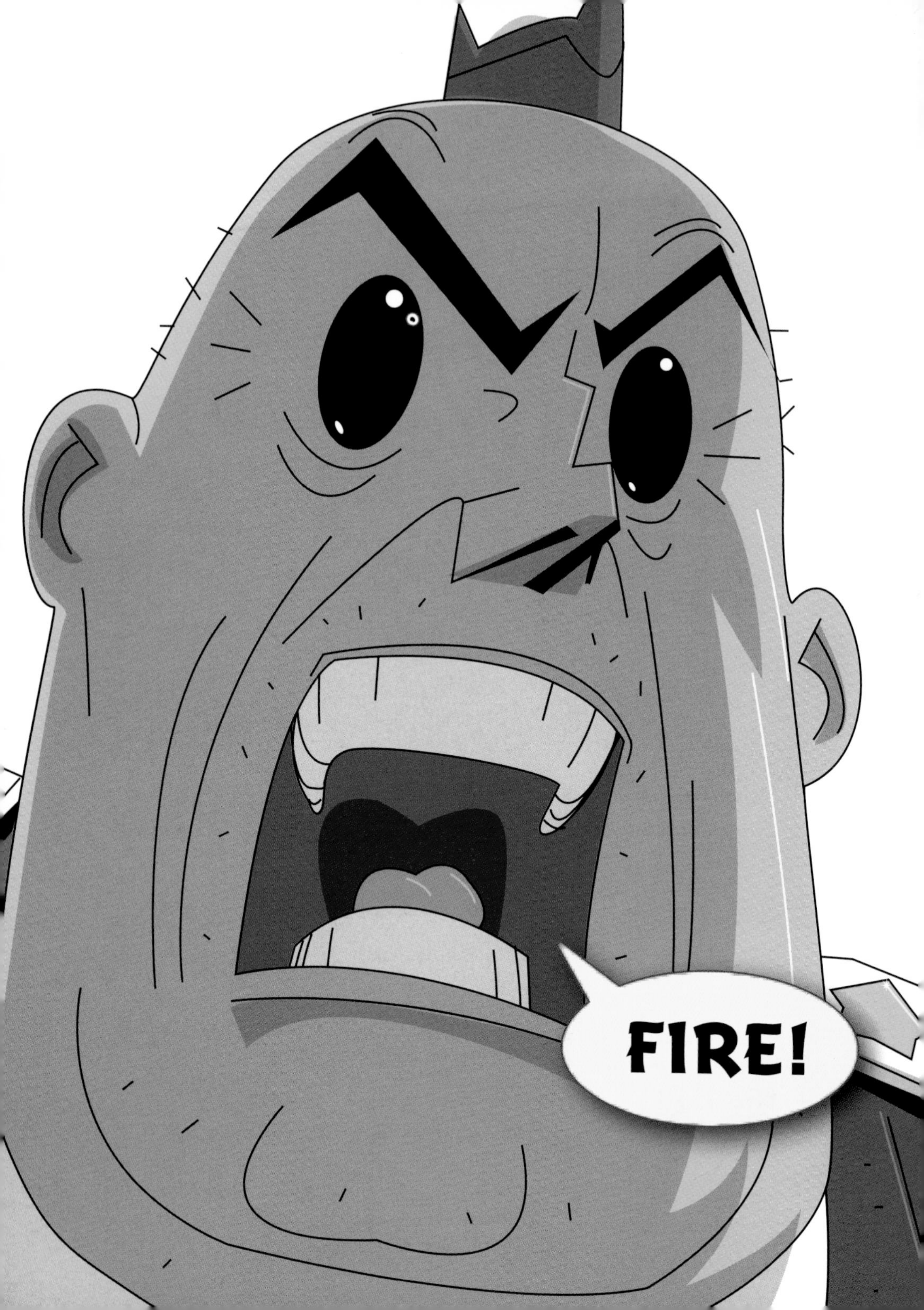
FIRE!

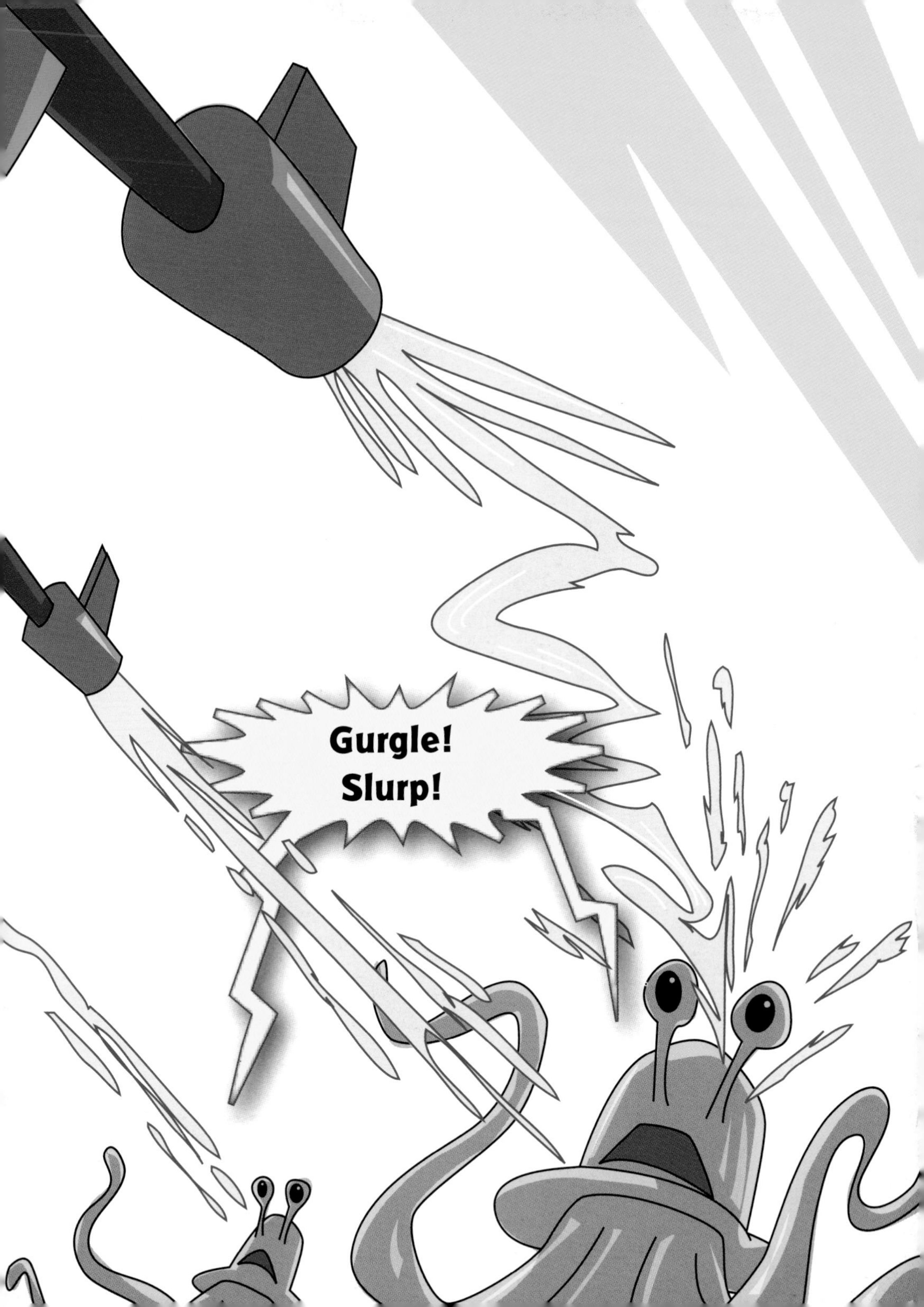
Gurgle!
Slurp!

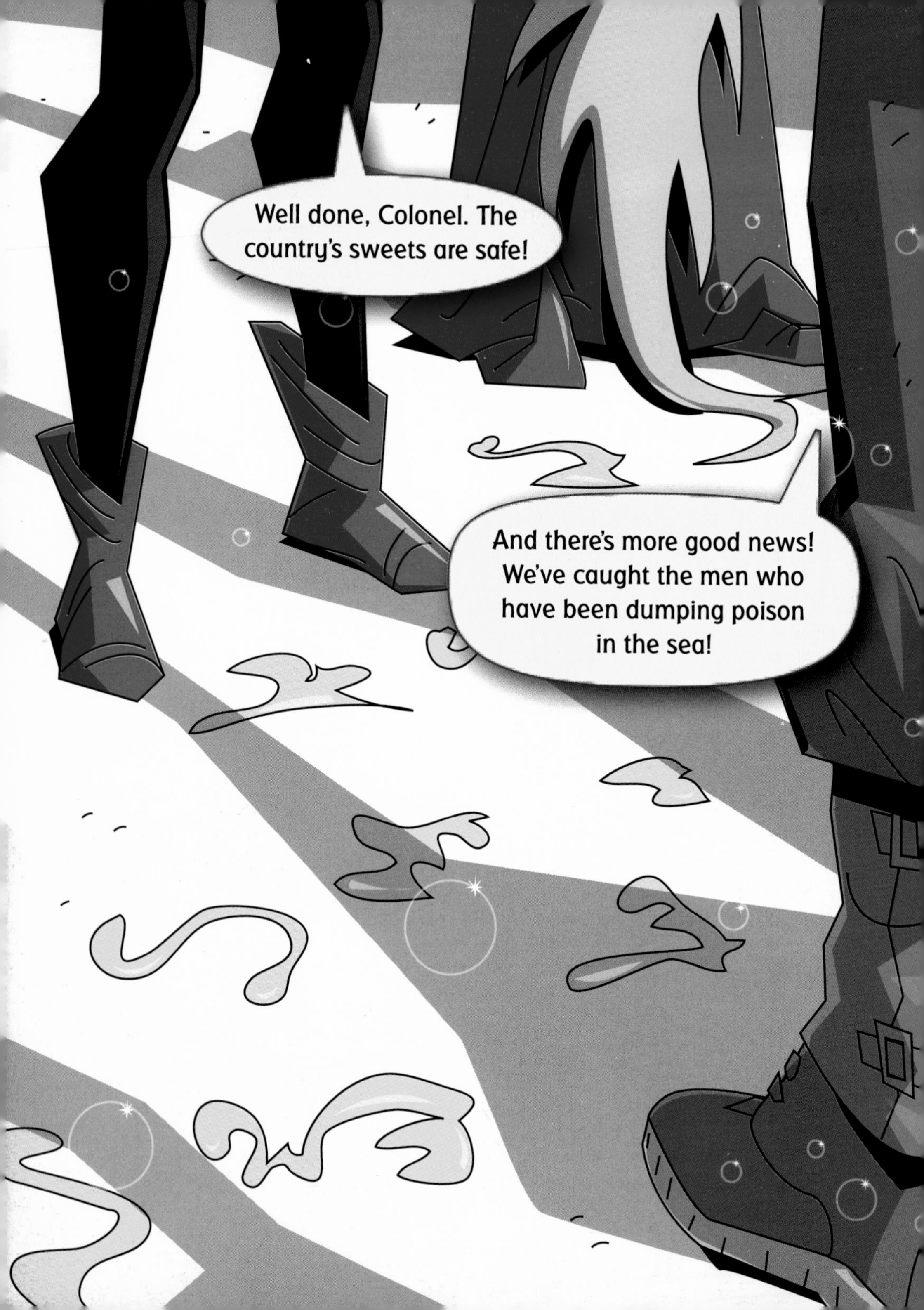
Well done, Colonel. The country's sweets are safe!
And there's more good news! We've caught the men who have been dumping poison in the sea!

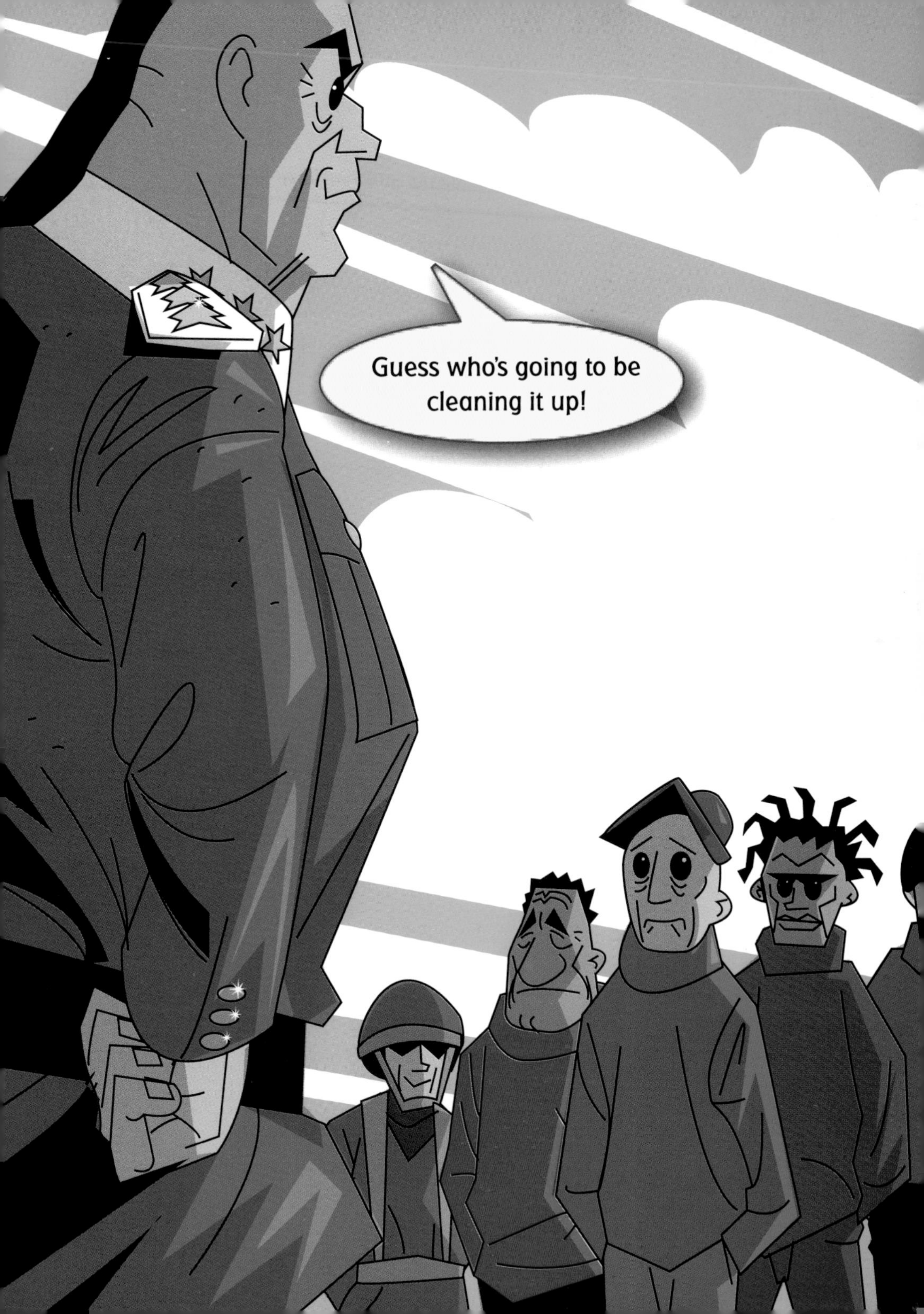
Guess who's going to be cleaning it up!

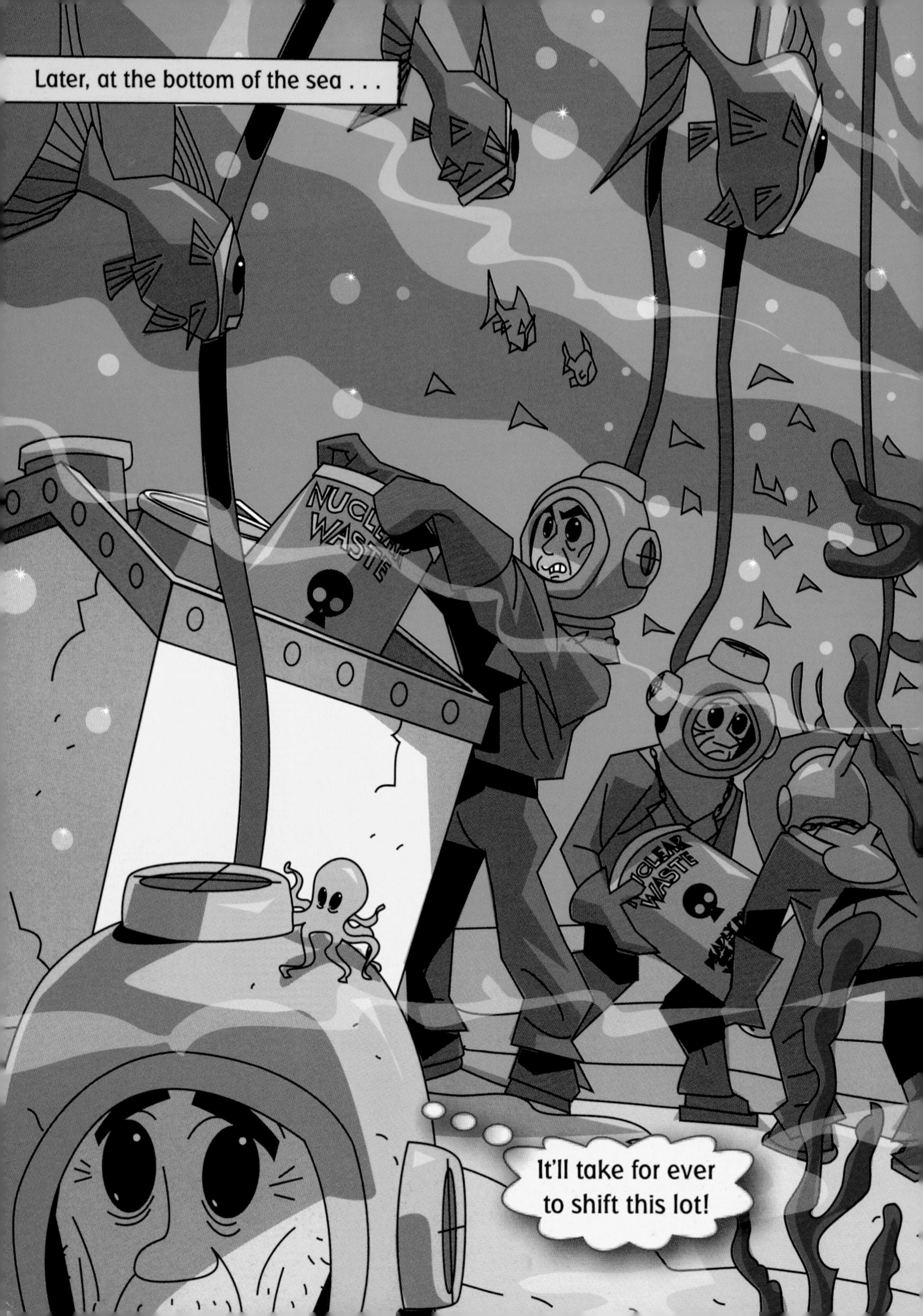
Later, at the bottom of the sea . . .
NUCLEAR WASTE
NUCLEAR WASTE
It'll take for ever to shift this lot!

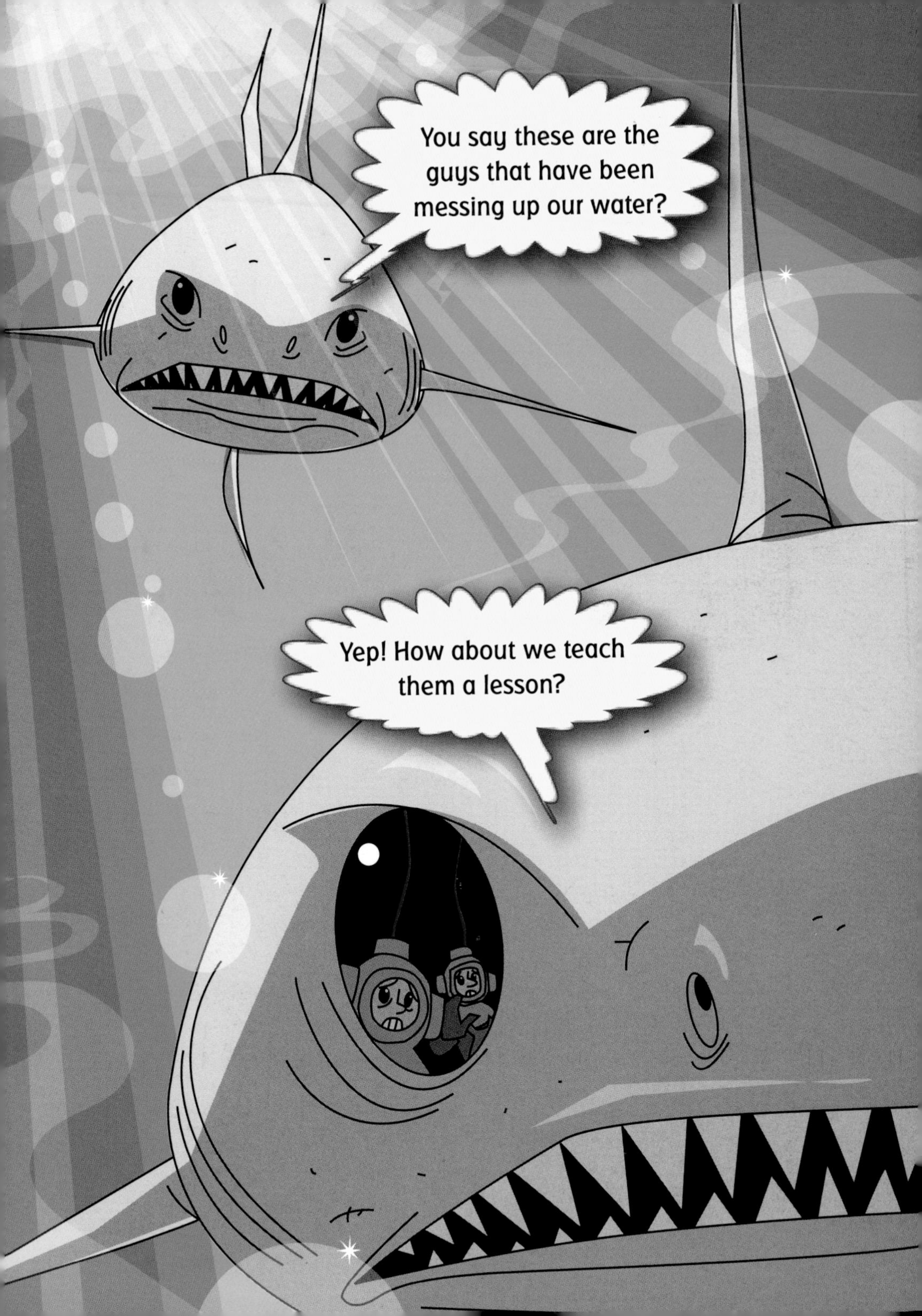
You say these are the guys that have been messing up our water?
Yep! How about we teach them a lesson?

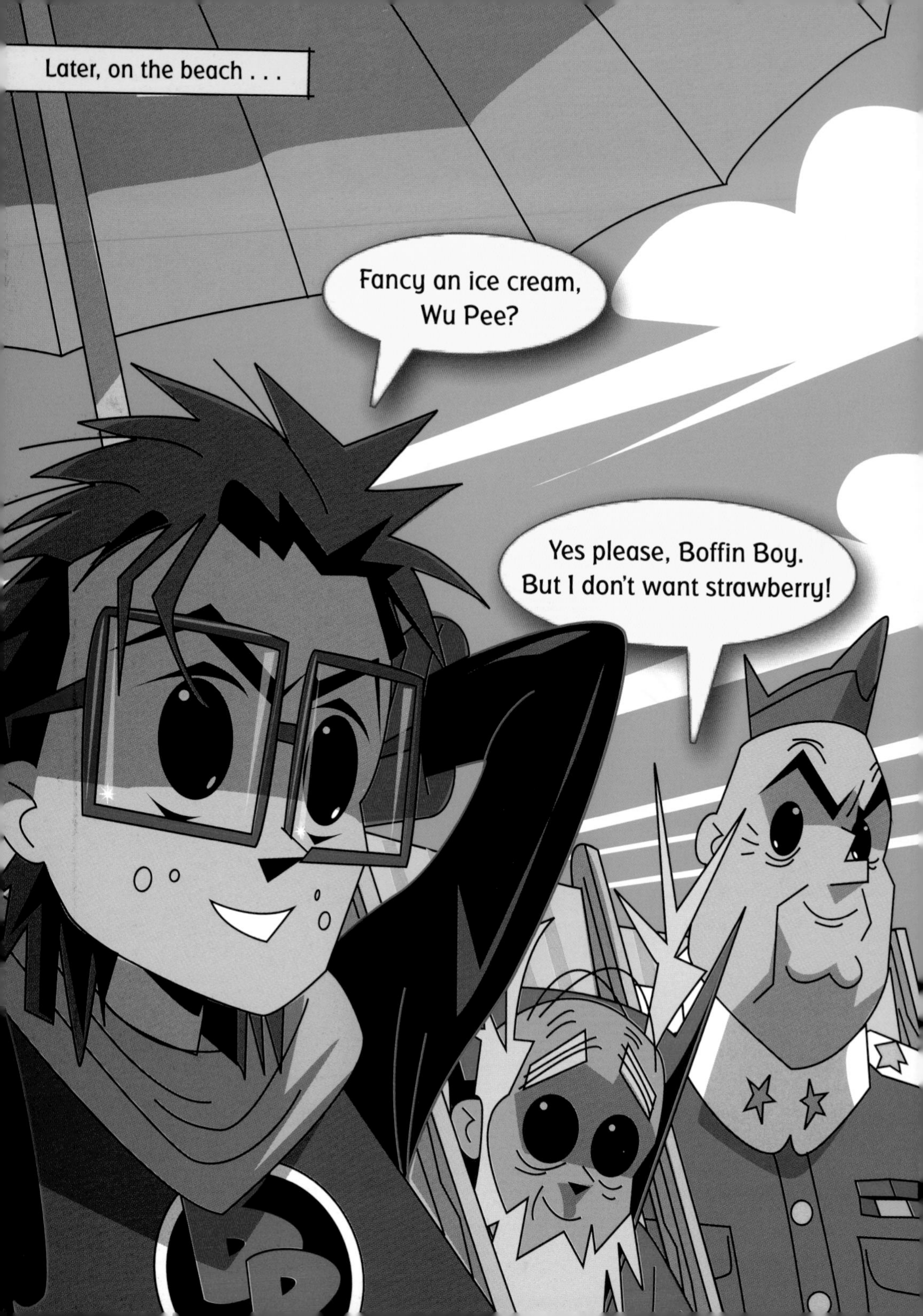
Later, on the beach . . .
Fancy an ice cream, Wu Pee?
Yes please, Boffin Boy. But I don't want strawberry!

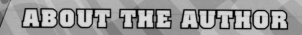

ABOUT THE AUTHOR

David Orme has written over 200 books
including poetry collections, fiction and
non-fiction, and school text books. When he
is not writing books he travels around the UK,
giving performances, running writing workshops
and courses.

Find out more at:
www.magic-nation.com.